The Matchmaker's Memo

RUBY D. FLOWERS

For rights and permissions, please contact: Rubydflowers@gmail.com

ISBN: 979-8-9921284-1-3

Chapter One

Hendrick Pfeiffer opened the door to his office and gazed over the bent heads, diligently typing away or staring at their monitors, desperately hoping to give the illusion of being industrious. Typically, his employees thought he didn't know what they were doing or that he was in full apprehension of the amount of time that they all spent on socials or internet shopping. Most of them were terrified of the man with the gruff voice and the overly enthusiastic laughter that rang out at the most inopportune times. For example, on the day that Casey, one of his junior executives, found out that his future ex-fiancé was cheating on him, Hendrick stood laughing riotously as tears slid down Casey's cheeks silently. Or that time that Chaundra, from the next department over, discovered that her best friend and her boyfriend of ten years suddenly realized that he liked boys a lot more than he liked girls. There stood Mr. Hendrick Pfeiffer, enraptured by giggles.

One could argue that he just happened to be laughing at the same time these unfortunate events had been revealed. However, one would be wrong. Hendrick kept a disturbingly keen awareness of everything that went on with his employees. Hendrick had an awareness of everything that went on at his baby, WCP Industries. His desire to direct and control his environment started early in his life. First, as a child, he was cast as a tree in his elementary school pageant. It didn't take long before he was telling his classmates what to do and became his teacher's right-hand man as director in training. From that point forward, Hendrick moved and directed people around in his day-to-day life like they were players on a screen or stage built just for him. In fact, Hendrick loved the drama and excitement of directing so much that he started his own production company while in college, Wild Cheetah Productions. It's a little-known fact, but that is exactly what WCP stands for. As he began to make connections for funding and sponsorship, Hendrick discovered that he had a gift for business, and gradually, the business side took precedence over his desire to make movies. He discovered that as the CEO of a corporation, he could have the ability to direct the outcome of so many characters. The opportunities were limitless! With the right connections and a few good product ideas, Hendrick was in business. He kept the name of the company hidden and led with the initials WCP. He never wanted to forsake his theatrical roots. He had a plan for his company, now a mega-corp, and for his workers. He had a plan for each and every one of them. Today was no different.

From: Kathy Starnes (on behalf of Hendrick Pfeiffer, CEO)

To: WCP Department Lead Distribution List

Subject: Quarterly Leadership Jam

Dear Colleagues,

As you all are aware, we at WCP like to develop our leadership on and off the shop floor through various team-building exercises and events. We were so successful last year with the quarterly events that I have decided to up the ante. We will now hold events bi-monthly, and you will be partnered with a fellow lead as I see fit. Please be prepared to attend each event, as they are mandatory. Each event will last anywhere from an evening up to four nights. In the event that you will be engaged for more than one night, all accommodations will be paid for by WCP.

Attached is the list of partners for our first event in two weeks. Please reach out to your teammates and get familiar with each other.

Sincerely,

Hendrick Pfeiffer, CEO

WCP Industries

The office was buzzing with chatter as the unsuspecting department leads opened their emails. A collective intake of breath was heard as they all realized that they were going to be beholden to their CEO even more frequently than they had been the year before. It was one thing to work for the man occasionally and commit to a team-building experience four times a year. Now, he had doubled the obligation and had threatened to take up multiple long weekends, engaging in company activity. The employees were dedicated, but this was a bit much even for them.

Casey felt dread slowly coat his insides as he opened up the attachment file to see who he would be partnered with. If it was Peter from accounting, he would have to punch something. That man had slept with Casey's fiancé. Once the engagement was broken, he tossed Kerry to the side like yesterday's garbage. Peter had only enjoyed the affair as long as he knew he was getting over on someone.

Casey exhaled as he saw the name Chaundra Jenkins next to his. He vaguely knew the woman. She worked over in Printing and Proofreading. If he remembered correctly, she was petite and curvy. She was memorable because of the brilliant colors she always wore, rich winter jewel tones, and vibrant brights in the spring and summer. She was eye-catching even in the few passing moments that he spent in her presence, whether it was in the elevator or grabbing a coffee in the breakroom. Her smile was as dazzling as the colors that popped against her skin. She was pretty, very pretty.

Two aisles down and through a glass door, Chaundra read her email details. Mr. Pfeiffer had paired her with Casey, a man she only knew about through the WCP rumor mill. She had heard about the drama between him, Kerry, and Peter. She remembered all of the turmoil that surrounded the situation. Kerry, his ex-fiancé, had shamelessly flaunted her relationship with Peter in front of Casey. She giggled at Peter's every word, running her hands down his back in the breakroom and stealing kisses in the hallway. Kerry had no shame. Most of the time, she was in full view of Casey's desk. Chaundra understood his sense of betrayal very well. Thankfully her ex didn't work with her, so she didn't have to see him making house with his new flame, but the sense of hurt, betrayal, and disbelief was still palpable for her. She had been nursing her own broken heart at the time and had felt a bit of kinship with Casey. Not that she ever reached out to him or said anything. He didn't know her from a can of paint and she was certain that he didn't need to know how much gossip was going around about his failed love life. It was bad enough that Hendrick had laughed when the whole situation had become public knowledge.

Chaundra rolled her chair back and poked her head into the cubicle next to her.

"Psss! Rachael! Have you opened your email yet?" she asked. Rachael was her best friend in the office.

"I did. I'm not happy about it. At. ALL." Rachael replied, sliding her chair back so that they were both halfway in the aisle of their section of the office.

"Oh no! Who did you get stuck with, Rach?"

Rachael rolled her eyes and hung her head. "Peter 'Sleazoid' Kane" How about you?"

"Ewww... you better watch out for him. You know he thinks he's everything to women. My partner shouldn't be too bad, but what a strange coincidence. I have Casey Travers."

"The one that Peter home-wrecked?" Rachael asked.

"The very same. I hope he won't be a downer the whole time," Chaundra said.

"And at least he's eye candy. All that thick curly hair, broad shoulders, and those eyes! That man is delectable! I don't know what that Kerry woman could have been thinking." Rachael said, staring dreamily in the direction of Casey's department.

"Yeah, she was so brazen with it. Oh, shoot! Hendrick is coming!" Chaundra replied.

Quickly, they scooted back to their desks. Chaundra put her head down and focused on a spreadsheet on her monitor. She didn't want Mr. Pfeiffer coming and stopping in their aisle. It's always best to be off the boss's radar. Chaundra poked her head out just as he passed their aisle, letting a sigh of relief start to escape when she saw that he had turned around and locked his piercing, steely grey eyes on her. He stood there staring over the cubicles, focused on Chaundra. She felt like squirming but was transfixed, like he had a powerful, inexplicable hold on her. Chaundra glanced from side to side, hoping to see him look at anyone but her. Unfortunately, he was still staring with a gleeful smirk and a sparkle in his eye. He arched his eyebrow and gave Chaundra the nod. Then he turned and stridently walked away to continue his tour of the floor.

"Rachael! Rach!!!" Chaundra whisper screamed.

"Girl, what?"

"I think I'm in trouble," she told Rachael about the moment that she and Mr. Pfeiffer had just shared.

"Shit! What did you do, Chaundra? You're on his radar now. What do you think it means?"

"I have no idea."

She really didn't have any idea. All she knew was that she was in for it now.

Chapter Two

From: Kathy Starnes (on behalf of Hendrick Pfeiffer, CEO)
To: WCP Department Lead Distribution List
Subject: Quarterly Leadership Jam (Update)

Dear Colleagues,

As you are aware, you have been selected to participate in the bi-monthly leadership jam. Attendance is not optional. Please be prepared to stay at the office overnight for this immersive event. I have many activities prepared and I hope you took full advantage of the time to introduce yourselves to your partner for the duration of this year's activities.

Pajamas are not optional!

Sleeping facilities and snacks will be provided. Everyone should arrive at the company auditorium at 5:30 p.m. Do not be late.

Sincerely,

Hendrick Pfeiffer, CEO

WCP Industries

Casey glanced around the auditorium nervously. The company email had thrown him for a loop. He knew that the potential for an overnight activity was high, but he didn't really expect the program to start off with an overnight event. He spotted Chaundra and decided now was the perfect time to make his introduction. She was standing off to the side of the auditorium speaking with another woman with an edgy half shaved head. Her friend was pretty in a punky sort of way, but Chaundra was downright beautiful. Her hair cascaded down her back in wavy, thin sister locs. The tips of her locs were a rose gold color, and she had bits of gold jewelry woven throughout her hair. Her curvy figure was plump in the best way. She was dressed in a jade green v-neck blousey dress that cascaded over her curves. Somehow, even though she was standing still, the fabric seemed to flow and ripple across her body like water until it came down to her hips, where it clung to the curve of her backside like a man clinging to salvation. Casey was startled by his reaction to her. He wasn't immune to beauty. However, when she turned her large, almond-shaped, chocolate-brown gaze on him, he felt like he was sucker punched, but in the best way possible. He had to get himself together if he was going to be stuck with this woman for the next twelve months.

"Hi, Chaundra? I'm Casey." The words stumbled out of Casey's mouth quickly, and he hoped that he didn't come across like an awe-struck teenage boy.

Chaundra gave him a warm smile. "Hi, Casey, you found me." Chaundra extended her hand, and Casey accepted it in a quick hand-shake. The husky velvet of her voice tickled Casey's ears.

"So, I guess we're partners," he said. He was at a loss for words.

"Attention. Ladies and gentlemen, can I get your attention, please? Please welcome your CEO, Mr. Hendrick Pfeiffer." The voice of Kathy Starnes came across the PA system and everyone in the room redirected their focus. Kathy stood tall and narrow, her gaze piercing the crowd, daring the group of employees to defy her. If Hendrick Pfeiffer was intimidating because he seemed to take a disproportionate amount of joy in the discomfort of his workers, Kathy was even more fearsome. Her back was ramrod straight, and her voice brooked no nonsense. It was easy to assume that even Mr. Pfeiffer would kowtow to her if she deemed it necessary to put him in his place.

Hendrick stepped forward, his cheeks rosy with excitement.

"People, I am so glad to have you here with me today to celebrate this new era at WCP. We are going to move mountains this year. You have been hand selected by me, personally, to accomplish the goals of our firm. With this in mind, I hope you all know how to follow instructions." He gazed out at his employees. It felt as though he was making eye contact with each and every one of them. "Not only are we going to team build, but we are going to have fun! If it's the last thing we do, it will be fun." He raised his eyebrows up and down in the way that people do to let you know there's more going on than the surface meaning of the words being spoken.

Chaundra nudged Casey and whispered, "Why do I feel like we're all collectively being threatened?"

Casey let a bark of laughter escape at her words. "Because we are," Casey replied.

Hendrick cleared his throat as his eye darted to the back of the auditorium where Casey and Chaundra stood.

"Ahem, with fun in mind, let us begin our first task. We're going to have a SLUMBER PARTY! So why don't you all scurry off, get in your jammies, and meet me back here in twenty minutes! Chop, chop!" He clapped his hands to emphasize his decree.

Everyone around Casey and Chaundra scattered.

"He can't be serious, can he?" Casey asked.

"I'm pretty sure he is. Let's just go and get this over with," Chaundra replied.

Twenty minutes later, everyone had returned to the auditorium dressed in modest sleepwear that ranged from t-shirts and basketball shorts to the standard button-down tops and pants set that have been worn for decades.

"Ah, very nice!" Hendrick said from the stage. He was dressed in a satin smoking jacket trimmed in velvet. Underneath his jacket, he wore a sheer, black, skin-tight shirt and black satin shorts that stopped at his knees. The shorts were trimmed in lace.

"Well, that is not at all what I expected," Chaundra whispered. "So pretty in lace!"

"Shhhh!" Casey replied. "You're going to get me in trouble again."

Chaundra's only reply was a wink at Casey.

"Since we're having a sleepover, I thought it would be fun if we played some games. I have two activities planned to break the ice. Can you guess what they are?" Hendrick looked over at the crowd. No one responded. "Remember, participation is mandatory."

A woman towards the front of the group raised her hand timidly.

"You there, Rebecca Winthrop, right? What do you think we're going to play?"

"Um, maybe that Ten Things in Common game?" Rebecca replied.

"Seriously, Rebecca? Where is your imagination? Do I look like a boring man?" Hendrick peered down at her. "I do not!"

"Of course not, sir," Rebecca squeaked out.

"Ladies and gentlemen, we are going to play *Seven Minutes in Heaven*!"

There was an audible gasp. Thirty pairs of eyes glared back at Hendrick.

"I, I can't do that. I have a boyfriend." "What is going on? Is this HR-approved?"

All sorts of questions went through the crowd.

"Relax people. This is a place of business. I expect you to go off and spend seven minutes *really* getting to know each other. Each selected team will go off together in an office, and there will be a list of questions that will help you get to know one another. All you have to do is get to know each other privately. Anything else that happens in those offices, well, hehehe, that's on you and whatever you consider heaven," Hendrick said.

"All right now," Kathy said, stepping up to the podium dressed in a hot pink satin pajama set. "Let's form a circle and get down to business. Once everyone is in place, I'll spin the bottle to pick the first team. Let's go, people."

Nervous giggles floated around the room as people sat down in a circle and prayed that the bottle would not point in their direction. Kathy kneeled in the center of the circle and gave the bottle a spin. Naturally, it pointed at Casey and Chaundra.

"Okay, you two, off you go, and don't do anything I wouldn't do," Hendrick said as he winked at his two employees.

Chapter Three

SEVEN MINUTES IN HEAVEN

"What is going on?" Casey asked once he and Chaundra were safely out of earshot of their boss.

"No, seriously. What have we been subjected to? This can't be normal professional behavior, right?" Chaundra asked.

"Absolutely not, but I do know I need this job. Let's just get through these questions and survive this round. Maybe he's just trying to shock us into immediate camaraderie?"

"Man, I hope so. Okay, let's do this thing," Chaundra replied.

"I've got to say, this is not what I expected while I was working so hard in college. Go to an Ivy League school, they said." Casey trailed off.

"Right? All I heard was Black Excellence, keep striving." Chaundra chuckled.

"Get into the right honor society, and I did all that just to find out I need to have a slumber party at work to *hopefully* be a success." Casey shook his head and took in their surroundings.

Heaven, or rather the office that was used by anyone who happened to be visiting from out of town, was sparsely decorated with the typical office furniture. However, in addition to the high-backed desk chair and overhead cabinetry, the desk was dotted with softly glowing votive candles, and the desk lamp had a sheer lavender scarf draped over it, giving the room a soft and oddly romantic glow. Center stage on the desk was a list of questions. Chaundra picked up the list and gasped.

"What is it?" Casey asked.

"You're not going to believe this." Chaundra handed this list over to Casey.

"How can this be possible? I thought this was a game of chance?"

At the top of the page, in bold lettering, were the following words, "Chaundra and Casey's Seven Minutes in Heaven."

"Well, if that isn't extremely creepy, I don't know what is. Let's get on with this," Chaundra said as she started to scan the page. "Ready for the first question?"

"Sure."

"Okay. Describe your first kiss. What would your perfect kiss be like?"

"What does kissing have to do with work? This is super weird. Let me see these questions."

Casey started reading down the list of questions, and as he read, his cheeks started to redden.

"Chaundra, I don't think we have to do this. He can't make us. These questions are really intrusive. He wants us to share our most recent heartbreak experience. We make paper and stationary, for crying out loud. I don't see how this is team building at all."

Light jazz suddenly began playing in the office, and Hendrick's voice came over the intercom.

"Remember, participation is mandatory. Have fun and answer the questions." Hendrick giggled.

Feeling helpless and freaked out, Chaundra decided to dive in and start answering the questions.

"Right, first kisses. I was a late bloomer. I didn't have kisses in middle or high school. I was kind of nerdy. My first kiss was actually my freshman year of college. It was awkward, tasted of beer and cigarettes, and was generally unpleasant. It was just some aggressive guy from my lit class taking advantage at a party. Definitely nothing special. How about you?"

"My first kiss was with Ellie Jacobs. We were eleven years old and she chased me after school in a game of freeze tag. Instead of tagging me "it," she cornered me behind the bike shack and kissed me. Regardless of the freeze tag or not, I was frozen in place. I couldn't believe she had kissed me. She was the prettiest girl in school, and all of the boys talked about how pretty she was. I felt like I was on top of the world."

"Aww, that's sweet! So much better than mine. I can just picture a little sixth-grade version of you. Curly hair flopping in your eyes. I bet you were a cutie!" Chaundra replied, grinning. "Now, tell me what your perfect kiss would be like."

"Given our current situation, you could say I peaked early," Casey said with a wry smile.

Casey fidgeted with the collar of his shirt and ran his fingers through his wavy hair before speaking.

"Soft, plump lips hovering closely to mine, whispered words, and maybe a slight giggle as our mouths begin a game of advance and retreat. Then, we come together as electricity and warmth make a complete circuit, joining our bodies in a playful dance. Tongues touching, swirling around each other, speaking more than words, promising future delights."

Chaundra began snapping and cheering.

"Damn, boy! Now I want to kiss you! I didn't know you were a poet like that. I can't even begin to compare with that description of a perfect kiss. I can never think of a perfect first kiss any other way," Chaundra said as she fanned herself dramatically.

"No fair! It's your turn. Tell me what you would like," Casey said, his eyes meeting hers with intensity.

"Okay, okay. My perfect first kiss would come after a wonderful date. Maybe we would go see a play or a lovely long walk along the waterfront. We would stop and look at the moon, listen to the lapping of the water, and our hands would find each other. We could stand there just holding hands and enjoying the closeness of the moment. And just when I least expected it, I'd feel his other hand reach up to touch my cheek and turn my face to his. Our eyes would meet, and we both would just know. And then we would kiss," Chaundra said and sighed, staring dreamily into the distance at a scene of her imagination.

The flames of the candles flickered and cast Chaundra in a golden glow. Casey couldn't resist looking at her, consuming the dreamy expression on her face. He could get lost staring at her. Her beauty was something that he could not pin down. All of the typical descriptors fell short of capturing what he saw on her face. Her brown skin shone like freshly cast bronze in the firelight. She was otherworldly. In the back of his mind, there was a niggling feeling that he was being rude by staring and also that he was supposed to be doing more than admiring this woman that he had just met. A knock sounded at the door, disrupting his reverie.

"Times up! Come back and join the circle," Kathy Starnes' voice broke through the enchantment of their shared experience.

The moment was shattered.

"We didn't get to the second set of questions," Chaundra said. "Do you think they'll know?"

"Nah, I mean, they weren't in here with us. At least we did part of it. This whole situation was unreasonable to begin with."

They stood and walked to the office door, their fingers brushing over each other as they both reached for the door.

"Oh, sorry," Chaundra said and pulled her hand back. Casey's hand had felt warm and strong under her touch.

"Ladies first," Casey said as he opened the door.

Chaundra walked through the door with Casey close behind her. The ghost of his touch lingered on her fingertips. As they entered the common space, she could feel her cheeks heat and flush.

"Where, where did everyone go?" Chaundra stammered.

The auditorium was nearly empty, save for Hendrick and Kathy.

"Did you think you were the only two to go to heaven?" Hendrick said, giving them a leering smile. "You were just the first. Everyone gets the same seven minutes. Seeing as you were the first, how was it?"

"It was fine," Casey answered cautiously.

"Well, what did you learn about each other? Anything... nice?" Hendrick asked.

"Oh, stop it now. You're making them nervous." Kathy interjected. "Besides, the others are starting to come out now anyway."

The rest of their co-workers began to trickle into the auditorium. Many of them had flushed faces or had their eyes cast downwards in embarrassment. Chaundra searched the crowd for Rachael. She found her scowling and walking hurriedly into the room. It looked as if she was trying to shake someone. Glancing behind Rachael, Chaundra found Peter smoothly walking behind Rachael with a Cheshire grin on his face. Chaundra couldn't wait to hear what had happened with them.

"Okay, friends, now that we've gotten that out of the way, check your emails for this weekend's assignments. You will spend the rest of the weekend working together on this project. I look forward to seeing your progress," Hendrick said.

"Let's go to my office to check our email," Casey said and led Chaundra to his area. Once inside, they were surprised to see two sleeping bags and two sets of pillows on the floor, side by side, on a camping mattress pad.

"I guess these are the sleeping accommodations, then," Chaundra huffed.

Casey just shook his head in disbelief. He pulled up his email and read aloud the following:

"Congratulations! You have successfully completed the first activity. Your next assignment will be a real treat! I dare you to say otherwise. Please see the file attached."

Casey opened the attachment.

"This motherf'er," Casey said under his breath.

"What? Is it a scavenger hunt?"

"I wish. He wants us to play Truth or Dare. He's already chosen the questions and the dares for us. We can either collect points by following through on the dares or give a report at the end of the weekend on our "Truths," Casey said.

"It can't be that bad, right? This is a corporation, after all," Chaundra said.

"If you say so. Do you want to go first? Truth or Dare?"

"Truth," Chaundra replied.

"You asked for it. The first question is what color underwear are you wearing right now?" Casey said and covered his face with his hands. "I'm so sorry. I swear this is the first question. Look for yourself."

"Motherf'er, indeed," Chaundra whispered. "Okay, what the hell, it's just clothing."

Chaundra pulled the waistband of her PJs aside and looked down. "Electric blue," she said.

Casey found himself peaking to catch a glimmer of the electric blue fabric. Quickly, he averted his eyes back to his monitor.

"Ahem. Here, I'll take a truth, too. For the solidarity," Casey said as he cleared his throat.

Chaundra walked over to stand next to Casey and clicked on the next question.

"Which do you prefer- Hanky or Panky?" Chaundra read and burst into giggles. "This is too absurd. Is there even a difference?"

Casey started to laugh, too. "If I didn't know any better, I would think Mr. Pfeiffer is a little sex obsessed. I don't even know how to respond to this."

"Google," Chaundra said, giggles still percolating forth.

"Okay," Casey pulled out his phone. "Hey, Google. What is the difference between Hanky and Panky?"

"Panko, Panko Flakes, are a Japanese style bread crumb." The AI voice responded. "Hanky, or handkerchief, is a small, often rectangular piece of fabric used as a substitute for a tissue."

Chaundra started to laugh in earnest and leaned on Casey's arm for support. "That ain't it! Ask again."

"Hey, Google. What is Hanky Panky?" Casey asked again, fighting the pull of his lips from turning into a full-fledged grin.

The AI voice of Google proceeded to answer. "Hanky Panky is a colloquial term used to speak of illicit activity, primarily sexual in nature. For example: The woman divorced her husband because she caught him having hanky panky with his secretary.:"

Chaundra couldn't take it and collapsed into Casey's arms in giggles. Rather than letting her slide to the ground, Casey wrapped his arms around her and pulled her close to him as he slumped into his chair. The two coworkers continued to giggle together until they had to catch their breath. The foolishness of the entire situation left them encapsulated in the moment. Casey found himself staring into Chaundra's deep chocolate-brown eyes. The laughter and breath caught in his throat, and all he could do was look into her eyes. In that moment, they both saw something in each other's gaze that they were too afraid to define. It was far too early to see or feel something like... like that.

"I guess we have our answer," Chaundra whispered.

"Answer?" Casey repeated back in confusion."

"Hendrick is a little sex obsessed," she replied.

The mention of sex brought the current state of things directly to Casey's attention. He was holding the most beautiful woman in his arms on his lap. The evening had gone in a surprising direction, and Casey found himself drawn to Chaundra. He only hoped that the physical manifestation would not become blatant to the gorgeous woman on his lap with the luscious curves.

"I guess he is." Casey shifted the temptation on his lap. His gaze drifted down to her lips.

"Well?" Chaundra asked. "What's your answer? Hanky or Panky?"

"A little hanky, a little panky. I think we can both agree- hanky panky is fun for everyone," he answered, voice huskier than it had been before.

Casey thought he was being suave with his answer, but Chaundra's reaction quickly corrected his thoughts. Her laughter peeled out like the tolling of multiple bells on a spring day. It was both refreshing and also frustrating.

"I'm sorry, I'm sorry. There was no way to answer that question and not sound douchey. We all love a little hanky panky," Chaundra said. At that moment, she realized that she was sitting on Casey's lap, cradled in his arms. Strong, thick arms that felt extremely capable and comfortable. Relishing the feeling, she began to become aware that not only was she seated in his lap, but her face was resting on his firm, broad chest. The rise and fall of his breathing was a soothing rocking motion that she could feel herself relaxing into until she fell asleep.

The sudden awareness of each other caused the two to become self-conscious. Feeling a need to pull back from the intensity of the moment, Casey started to stand up just as Chaundra pushed up and away from his lap. The end result of this spontaneous motion was that the normal momentum of their movements escalated exponentially, causing Chaundra to pitch forward onto the desk, hands splayed wide to catch herself and prevent a face plant. Simultaneously, Casey was thrust forward, his pelvis ending up pressed forward into Chaundra's backside. As he also attempted to prevent himself from falling, he grabbed her hips. Unfortunately for them, the mishap coincided with the unexpected opening of the office door.

"My, my, my," Hendrick said with a sigh. "You two really are getting to know each other very well. What would HR say?"

Casey and Chaundra both sputtered, trying to explain themselves.

"It's not what it looks like," Casey said.

"I was falling-" Chaundra added, trying to clear things up.

"None of that, now. You two don't have to explain what's right before my eyes. Truth or Dare seems to really be quite the icebreaker. Carry on, you two!" Hendrick grinned and exited the office with a firm slam of the door.

"Ughhh!!!!" Chaundra groaned. "Can today get any weirder?"

"I think we've done enough of the games for the night," Casey said, reluctantly releasing his grip on her hips. Something about touching Chaundra just felt instinctive, primal.

"You're right. If you don't mind, I'm just going to step out, maybe grab a bottle of water and call it a night. If there are any other tasks, I'll help. Otherwise, I'm going to turn in," Chaundra said.

"Yeah, no, I totally agree. We've made enough progress for one day," Casey replied.

The activities of the day had exhausted both of them. It was no wonder that they were both curled up in their sleeping bags by 8:30 p.m. At some point in the night, they worked their way toward each other, creating that perfect nighttime spoon. Casey's arm draped over Chaundra's waist. Each had a contented smile on their faces.

The door to the office slowly opened a crack. A familiar chuckle could be heard, and then the door was shut for the final time that night.

Chapter Four

MORNING AFTER

Chaundra basked in a cloud of spicy masculinity and heat. She couldn't remember sleeping so well in a long time. She felt the iron strength and safety of arms holding her closely as she slept. She loved every second of it. It was just too bad that it was all a dream. Chaundra knew that the reality was that her man had left her for his basketball buddy, Eric. She hadn't slept next to, let alone in the arms of a lover, in a long time. She was going to make this dream count. She wasn't going to wake up anytime soon. No, ma'am! Chaundra was no fool. She was going to take the loving, even if it was only the sensation of it in dreamland where she could get it. Chaundra sighed and nestled into those warm arms just a little bit closer.

Casey started to rouse from his night of rest. Sleep had never, ever, felt so good to him. He felt like he could take on the world and kick some serious ass! He knew it was all down to the woman who lay in his arms. He was confident that his love was always with him. She was his strength, and he was hers. He felt her nestle in a little bit closer and loved every touch of her body against his. Her curves were more luscious than usual, and he craved it. Sunlight pressed against his eyelids but he refused to open them just yet. He wanted more. More of this feeling of completeness. More of the sensation of this soft, feminine body against his. Kerry had left him, sure. He knew that was what would meet him when he gave up on sleep, but he could cuddle and embrace this dream woman a little bit longer before reality kicked him in the nuts.

"Wake Me Up! hehehe! Before you go, go!" Hendrick's off-key voice blared across the PA System, making everyone within the corporate retreat's eyes open immediately. "Wakey, wakey! You don't want to hear my high note. Good morning, boys and girls!" Hendrick ended his wake-up call with a long giggle.

Casey and Chaundra were pulled abruptly from self-delusion to reality in an instant. Each could feel the other's body tense up. Neither knew what to do. They were essentially waking up from the best sleep they had in the arms of a co-worker. No longer could they pretend they were asleep. Hendrick's announcement was forcing them into reality.

"Ahem. Good morning, Miss Jenkins," Casey said, stiff politeness taking over his voice. Gone was the warmth and attraction of the night before. Informality was out. He wanted to ignore the situation as much as possible.

"Good morning, Mr. Travers," Chaundra replied, equally stiff. She was keenly aware that her butt was flush against Casey's groin. She started to move her right hand only to find that her fingers were intertwined with his as his hand rested between her breasts. She also noticed that their breathing had synced up. His intake was her intake. Her exhale was his exhale. They were in perfect rhythm.

"Shall we face the day?" Chaundra asked after a moment. She couldn't figure out a way to extricate herself from this embrace. How had it even happened? All she knew was that they had both agreed to turn in for the night and had been in separate sleeping bags. She could admit that there had been a frisson of attraction last night, but she certainly wasn't so hard up that she needed to press her body against a veritable stranger, a work colleague, no less. All Chaundra knew was that she needed distance from this moment. Clarity could only come if she was no longer ensconced in Casey.

"Yes, I think we should. I'm sure there is another task ahead of us. Let me just..." Casey started to untangle their fingers and slide his body back from Chaundra. The sudden break in connection caused him to cringe internally. His body screamed that this was wrong. Thankfully, Casey had learned that he couldn't trust his body to make the best decisions.

"Of course," Chaundra replied as she pulled her hand away as well.

Once they were separated, Chaundra stood up, running her hand through her hair. She grabbed her toiletry bag and hurried to the office door.

"I think I'll head to the restroom," she said and hurried out before Casey could reply.

She found Rachael in the bathroom, staring blearily into the mirror.

"Chaundra," Rachael said, glancing up at her through the mirror's reflection. "It is so good to see you. I can't believe I had to be around that man for an entire evening! He is the absolute worst! I hope you had a better night than I did."

Chaundra smiled, relieved that something about this morning was finally getting back to normal.

"Peter was that bad, huh?" Chaundra asked as she pulled out her toothbrush and face wash.

"He really was," Rachael replied and then launched into a highly detailed description of all of the ways that Peter was obnoxious. Chaundra was delighted to have her attention pulled away from thinking about Casey, Casey's smell, his arms, and even his idea of a perfect first kiss. She was certain that she could forget about everything that had transpired. It was just a random fluke.

For his part, Casey was thankful to have his office to himself for a while. He needed some space. He had to pull himself together. From the moment he had seen Chaundra the previous evening, he was keyed up. To distract himself, he sent a text to his friend, Rome, and set up a poker game for later in the day. Then Casey went to the men's room and had the unfortunate chance to nearly run into Peter as he entered the facility.

"Watch it, little buddy!" Peter said and pushed past Casey, giving him a condescending leer. Just the nearness of Peter was able to drive all of the warm fuzzies of Chaundra away.

"I'm not your buddy," Casey growled.

Casey returned to his office and found Chaundra dressed in the same outfit from the previous night and seated in the guest chair, reading a file. From that point forward, the energy of last night had been fully pushed to the ether. Neither acknowledged what they had experienced and plunged ahead, business as usual. The rest of the weekend flew by in a far more work-appropriate fashion.

Chapter Five

TRUTH REPORT

From: Casey Travers
    CC: Chaundra Jenkins; Kathy Starnes
    To: Hendrick Pfeiffer

In a joint effort to build camaraderie and a cohesive workforce, Ms. Jenkins and I would like to submit our "Truth Report" for your review.

We would like to evaluate our newfound knowledge of each other on a five-point scale, with one being that we had no idea and that we are truly surprised, up to five points representing that we have discovered something both surprising and valuable to the team as a whole.

Honesty: 5 (Casey and Chaundra respectively)

Willingness to lean into Discomfort: 4

Compatibility: 4

Our overall assessment, based on the questions posed, was that both entities were capable people who could excel in any situation while randomly partnered.

Submitted for your approval,

Casey Travers, Associate Executive Director

Chaundra Jenkins, Associate Director

Casey hit the send button. He knew that the report was scant on information but there was nothing to be done about it. How much personal information did a company deserve to have? He hoped it would be enough to appease Mr. Pfeiffer. Before this year's team-building session, Casey would have said he worked in your typical corporate environment with a disconnected, disinterested CEO. However, this first experience that Mr. Pfeiffer created seemed oddly specific, down to the mood lighting.

Casey sat in his high-backed office chair, in his mid-size office that was a carbon copy of every junior executive office at WCP, and mused over just how interesting the previous weekend's event was. Chaundra Jenkins... he found himself thinking about waking up with her nestled so closely to his body. She felt so warm...

"Case, did you see the latest memo?" a nasal voice pierced through Casey's reverie. "What with the goofy grin?"

"Jacobson, didn't I tell you to knock before entering?" Casey asked, picking up a miniature basketball and tossing it at his colleague. "What memo?"

"There's an opportunity for two promotions. Ol' man Pfeiffer is looking to open up full executive positions." Jacobson replied as he dodged the ball and made a feeble attempt to catch the ball.

"Oh really? You actually have something interesting to share for once. That still doesn't excuse you barging in like a hyena with sinusitis."

"Don't allergy shame me. And I'm always bringing added value . You gonna go for it? You've been an associate exec. for a minute."

Casey felt a twinge of frustration that he fought to keep from his facial expression. He knew how long he had been languishing in the junior ranks. Sometimes, he felt like everyone knew. He was a failure of a son. He was the promise that never delivered. Even now, he could hear his ex, Kerry, sneering at him as she slammed the door in his stricken face. *Casey, did you expect me to sit around forever waiting for you junior ass? You're a disappointment all around. I deserve better than what you have to offer. I deserve someone who's actually going somewhere. Peter is going somewhere. Sorry if I'm hurting you, but the truth hurts.*

"No time like the present to make an advancement," Casey said, attempting a cocky grin.

"Right? You've got this man. You're lucky. You've got an edge to getting this promotion."

"How so?"

"You were selected to be in the Quarterly Leadership Jams. That's key. You get face time, and Pfeiffer implied that your performance and ability to "dazzle" in his challenges will give the candidates a leg up in the competition," Jacobson said. "I've got a 9:00. Catch you at the basketball court after work?"

"Yeah. I'll be there." Casey replied and turned to his desk. He had work to do if he was going to prove he was worthy of that promotion. Now was not the time to fantasize about a co-worker who smelled like sweet mango and coconut and had a warm, luscious body.

From: Kathy Starnes (on behalf of Hendrick Pfeiffer, CEO)

To: WCP Department Lead Distribution List

Subject: Quarterly Leadership Jam (Session Two Update)

Dear Colleagues,

Our last event was an astounding success. We work better when we know each other better. Your cooperation and willingness to put in the work, leaning into discomfort was commendable. We have something even better for our next event!

Please come prepared with a five-minute presentation about what you have learned from and about each other and how you believe your connection will improve WCP.

Don't get it twisted. We're going to have a great time! Workout attire is recommended.

Sincerely,

Hendrick Pfeiffer, CEO

WCP Industries

Insta-chat Travers: Hi, Chaundra. Did you see the email?

Insta-chat Jenkins: Hey, Casey! No, opening it now. Should I be worried?

Insta-Chat Travers: I'm not sure. Seems safe, but after last time...

Insta-chat Jenkins: Right? I'm feeling a little gun-shy. The only thing that worries me is that last bit about workout gear.

Insta-chat Travers: Why? You're fit.

Insta-chat Jenkins: Thanks *blush emoji*

Insta-chat Jenkins: Not everyone can be as buff as you. *winky emoji* I just don't want to have to run a 5k or something like that.

Insta-chat Travers: *cheese smile emoji* It can't be any worse than last time. We'll just have to find out on Friday. Team Travers-Jenkins for the win! *fist pump emoji*

Chapter Six

Friday afternoon found Casey, Chaundra, Rachael, and most uncomfortably, Peter Kane, all seated next to each other, waiting for the shoe to drop on the evening's assignment. Chaundra could feel the tension radiating off of Casey. It was unfair that he had to be in such close proximity to the douche who was instrumental in his heartbreak. They had yet to talk about what had happened between his fiancé and Peter, but Chaundra was confident that she could still show him some support. Chaundra rested her hand on Casey's knee. It was bouncing a mile a minute. He glanced over at her and she flashed him a reassuring smile. A thrill shot up Casey's spine as he smiled back, Chaundra's action momentarily distracting him from the man who seemingly ruined the life he had planned.

"Ladies and Gentlemen! What a delight it is to see you all," Hendrick addressed the crowd without any of the usual preamble from Kathy Starnes. Kathy stood behind him, wearing a sour expression and a surprisingly athletic body clad in Lululemon. Of course, in true Hendrick fashion, he wore skintight Lycra pants with a cheetah print stripe running down the side of the legs and a half-shirt made of netting. He would not have been out of place in a 1980s glam band. His version of athletics attire left much to be desired. "Today, we will have another wonderful interactive experience that will test your abilities to problem solve, work together as a team, and unravel uncomfortable situations."

Hendrick gazed out, smiling benevolently.

"Reach under your seats, please," Kathy interjected.

From under their seats, folks pulled out various parts of a game: a spinner, a tally sheet, and a folded mat.

"Please unfold the mat. I think you will all enjoy this one," Hendrick said with a giggle.

Chandra cringed at the sound. That giggle was beginning to haunt her dreams. Nothing good ever came after that sound. Peter happened to have pulled the mat and began to unfold it.

"As you can see, you have been grouped together as couples. These are your groups for this assignment," Kathy's crisp voice rang out.

Chaundra realized that her partner was going to be in hell. Being forced to work with Peter for the night could be really damaging to his soul. Her time with him at the last event and over the successive weeks demonstrated his gentle and kind nature. Without intending to, she turned and stared at Casey, taking in his features. She wondered what was going on in his mind as his jaw worked up and down, clenching in tension. His dark curls fell forward over his forehead. The ceiling lights pulled out russet highlights. He really was too beautiful. She hadn't fully grasped how attractive he was prior to being paired with Casey for teambuilding.

"This is bullshit!" Rachael gasped.

Chaundra pulled her gaze away from Casey.

"What? Oh my goodness!" Chaundra was caught off guard by the site before her. Peter was standing, holding up the mat. The grin on his face as he winked at Rachael was unsettling. Peter's green eyes sparkled like a cat eyeing a fresh bowl of cream.

"We're playing Twister, ladies." Peter arched his eyebrow as he focused his gaze on Rachael. "I can't wait to make a knot with you two —pretzel style. Love 'em, twist 'em, and leave 'em. That's my motto."

Casey grit his teeth and abruptly stood up.

"Excuse me, Chaundra. Rachael."

Chaundra watched Casey walk away, his shoulders hunched in aggravation.

"What's his problem?" Peter scoffed. "Some guys just don't know how to appreciate a good time when it's staring them in the face."

"Are you serious right now? You really are an asshole!" Chaundra said. "Rachael, I'll be back."

"I'll be alright. Take care of your partner." Rachael glared at Peter. As Chaundra followed after Casey, she heard Rachael say to Peter, "She's right, you know. You're such an asshole."

"But you wouldn't have it any other way," Peter laughed.

Chapter Seven

THE HALLWAY

"Casey, wait," Chaundra called.

Casey turned to see Chaundra gliding down the hallway toward him. He didn't want her to see the anguish on his face, so he turned away and looked out of the wall-to-ceiling window.

"Hey," Chaundra rested her hand on his shoulder. "Don't let Peter get to you. I know this can't be easy."

Casey laughed in frustration.

"What do you even know about it?"

"Not much, but I know heartbreak, and I know that Peter was a big part of yours."

"So what, the whole company knows?" Casey's frustration came through in the shake of his voice.

"It doesn't matter what the company knows. It's just gossip. What I know is that my partner is in pain." Chaundra's hand moved to Casey's back and began making soothing, circular motions between his shoulder blades. "And that's something that I don't like to see. You can talk to me if you want to. Or we can go and sit quietly on that bench over there and just be silent. Together."

Casey pulled in a slow, deep breath. "Can we just sit?"

"Sure."

Together, they walked down the hallway and settled down on a padded bench with a view of the city below.

"Thank you, Chaundra. I appreciate you."

"Any time. I'm serious."

The space between them seemed to shrink as they sat watching the cars pass on the street six stories down. The sun began to sink and the clouds started to glow in purples and pinks, adding a rich orange fire to the horizon. Without thinking, Casey and Chaundra's hands inched toward each other.

"You know, it's not the embarrassment that gets to me," Casey interrupted their solitude.

Chaundra nodded. "No, it's the loss of dreams, connection, and confidence. At least, that's how I felt when my fiancé left me."

"It happened to you, too?" Casey asked.

"It did. Turns out the man that was my best friend, confidant, and lover loved his homeboy a little bit more than me," Chaundra sighed.

Briefly, Chaundra's mind drifted back to her relationship with Joel. They had been each other's rock since her freshman fifteen. They had met in the laundry room of their co-ed dorm and bonded over her super-hero jammies. Retro-style Wonder Woman undies. She had just unloaded her dryer. She saw the hottie with a body begin to load the same machine with his wet laundry. Blushing, she gave the dark-eyed man a quick smile and started to duck out of the room with her bag of freshly laundered clothes.

"Hey, I think you forgot something." Chaundra knew he wasn't talking to her and kept walking. She heard footsteps getting closer, and a hand tapped her on the shoulder.

"Yo. Blue jeans, I think this might belong to you?"

Chaundra turned and was struck by his muscles and crooked smile.

"Wonder Woman, right?" He held the skimpy blue and white starred panties up by one finger.

"Oh my gawd..." Chaundra put a hand over her face and grabbed the garment.

"I bet they look real good on you. I'm Joel." He leaned in and whispered, "Don't worry. I have Wolverine pajamas. I get it."

"Yeah? But are you a true fan?"

"How about we find out over a cup of coffee at the Coffee Hub?" Joel raised his eyebrows.

From that point forward, Chaundra and Joel could always be found together. Perhaps it was because of everyone's expectations, but the two soon found themselves in an easy and comfortable relationship. Graduation came and went. They secured internships and entry-level jobs in the same city. It only made sense that they would move in together. While there was no intense passion, the couple were deeply devoted to each other. They came together intimately twice a week, and it was... nice. Chaundra could see herself living that life well into old age. Things changed once Joel got hired full-time. He needed to work later and later. He was assigned a special project with his co-worker, Brent. She noticed that Brent's name came up a lot in conversation but thought it was nice that Joel had made a solid friend. Chaundra had Mable and her other girls from uni.

Things began to change for the couple again. Suddenly, Joel wanted sex every morning before work. Chaundra wasn't complaining. It was a great way to start the day. She went to work smiling daily, so much so that Rachael had to comment on it. Joel proposed soon after the uptick in their sex life, and the future that Chaundra imagined seemed like it was coming true. She was ecstatic.

She had the shock of her life when she found text messages from Joel's best man, Brent, begging him to reconsider. Brent said that he knew Joel was lying to himself and that he would always be there, waiting for him. He loved him even if Joel wasn't ready to face it. They had something special if he would only admit it to himself.

Confronting Joel was the hardest thing that she had ever done. At first, he denied his true feelings, but then he broke down and cried. He loved her, he really did and he never betrayed her, never cheated, but he couldn't deny that he felt something for Brent that he never felt with any woman, not even her. She held him in her arms and comforted him through his tears as he realized that his whole life was a lie.

"Shhh... it's ok. I'm here for you." Chaundra told him.

It wasn't ok though. Who would be there for her as she sent out cancellations? Who would hold her as she cried alone because her best friend, her lover, could never truly love her back?

Casey and Chaundra's pinkies intertwined.

"You're wonderful, you know?" Casey glanced toward Chaundra. "He clearly had to discover himself. I don't know him, but what I know of you... it couldn't have been anything you did."

"Case, I'm here to comfort you!" Chaundra chuckled. "But thank you, and you know, whatever happened with Peter and Kerry, that was about her and not you either. She must have lost her mind."

"I wish. That would have made more sense to me. Then I wouldn't feel like my judgment and understanding were so off. Like, how could I not know it was all happening right in front of me?"

Chaundra slid a little closer. "Can I tell you a secret?"

Casey inched towards her. "Please do."

"There's nothing wrong with us. My ex and your ex, the issues were all their own. Nothing is wrong with our judgment. We have to learn to trust ourselves again, but I have confidence in us."

They were shoulder to shoulder, hip to hip now. Hands intertwined.

"And bottom line- you can be secure that you'll never be an asshat like Peter Kane. That's a win for you and the rest of the world. You have enough self-respect that you don't have to pick off of someone else's love plate. If nothing else, we can go back in that room, participate in Mr. Pfeiffer's bizarre team building, confident that you are the better man."

"He is an ass hat." Peter laughed. "Thank you for making me laugh."

They sat for a few moments longer, enjoying the feel of each other's warmth and the energy that was being drawn out from each of their hearts toward each other.

Distantly, the door to the auditorium creaked, a contented sigh drifted in the air. Things were falling into place.

"Should we-"

"I guess it's that time-"

They laughed as they both stood up.

"Yeah," Chaundra said. "We should probably head back in."

Casey's heart pounded in his chest. His feelings for Chaundra were going through a metamorphosis. Things were changing between the two of them. Even now, he realized that they had spent the greater part of their time away from the group hand in hand. Visions of her seated in his lap, of waking up spooned against her, even that brief moment in the office with his hand gripping her hips... everything spoke to his heart and a budding passion. He cleared his throat as he stepped closer to her, his eyes roaming over her features and settling on her lips.

"We really should go back, but I prefer being out here." He took a step closer. He could feel the rise and fall of her breasts against his chest. "With you."

Chaundra never realized how much she could want to comfort a man and, in the next moment, desperately wanted to kiss him. She couldn't do it though. This was a work assignment, not a setup for romance. She knew the look in Casey's eyes. He was feeling her, too.

"Casey, I think-" She was hushed by the whisper light sensation of Casey's lips against hers. Lost for words, she only wanted to feel that delicious pressure again. Despite her mind telling her to retreat, Chaundra pushed forward, seeking out a deeper kiss.

Casey couldn't believe what he had done and, for a microsecond, thought he ought to apologize, but then he felt Chaundra's mouth pressed against his. No time for second-guessing, he pulled her tightly into his arms and began to pour every emotion and desire he had at that moment into the kiss. Just as her lips parted and his tongue sought hers, that damned giggle could be heard coming from up the hallway.

They pulled away from each other instantly. Chaundra's fingers drifted to her lips.

"Let's get back before we're missed," Casey said, smiling. Chaundra nodded and allowed Casey to guide her back toward the auditorium, his hand resting on her lower back. The kiss seared into both of their memories.

Chapter Eight

TWISTED

U pon entering the auditorium, they were immediately bombarded by Rachael.

"You guys! This is pure insanity. Everyone's getting set up for this "Get to Know You" twister game. I'm so glad you're back. I did not want to play this alone... with *him*." Rachael gestured toward Peter.

"Also, it's not just a basic game of twister. There are personal questions and weirdo situations that we have to problem solve as we get ourselves all twisted up together." She blurted out in one breath.

"Yikes!" Chaundra replied. Secretly, she was glad Rachael came to them. It gave her the opportunity to step away from Casey and shake the warm, fuzzy cocoon that was forming around them. Chaundra was about that business and didn't want or need to deal with "feelings." Her ex, Joel, had been more than enough for her and that turned out miserably. She just wasn't ready to face all that came with what was growing between her and Casey. This was work, for crying out loud!

"Hold up, what's up with you? You look different." Rachael eyed her suspiciously and then glanced at Casey.

"Nothing is up," Chaundra replied, widening her eyes for emphasis.

"Hmph! Tell that to someone else. We'll be talking later about this." Rachael grabbed Chaundra's arm and pulled her back towards their seats. "You know, Casey has been looking pretty hot lately."

Rachael cut her eyes toward Chaundra to gauge her reaction. As she suspected, Chaundra's cheeks became flushed.

"Ummhmm.... we're definitely going to talk later."

"People!" Kathy Starnes called everyone to order. "Please, come to order! We will begin the problem-solving portion of today's team-building exercise now."

"Hehehe, yes indeed. Your task will be to answer our questions and then place yourselves on the corresponding color on the mat. You *will* get tangled up together, however you can win by learning to work together and strategically start placing your limbs. You can either work together as you get to know each other or stay resistant and fall into a tangled knot. You will all play at the same time." Hendrick's smile gleamed with merriment as he looked out upon his employees. His cheeks were rosy and cherubic.

"Okay. Everyone, lay your mats on the floor. Male-presenting employees stand on one side of the mat while female-presenting employees stand on the opposite side. Gender-fluid/neutral employees may choose where they want to be. The key is to have two people facing opposite two people. Let's see how well you all can follow directions."

Chaundra inwardly groaned. This positioning meant that Casey was going to have to stand side by side in alignment with Peter, his arch-nemesis. Hopefully, their talk, and maybe even the kiss (ugh! She couldn't believe she had indulged herself like that.) would be a suitable distraction for Casey. Their eyes met across the mat, and she saw a playful twinkle in his eye. She was relieved to see that he was going to be okay. If anything, she should have been more concerned about Rachael. Her bestie couldn't stand still. She was twitchy and looking everywhere she could except at the man who stood across from her. Meanwhile, Peter seemed to have a mono-focus, and it was latched on to Rachael. A devilish grin laced his, unfortunately, handsome face.

"Hey, do I need to worry about you two?" Chaundra asked.

"Nah, I'll be alright. Peter just needs to stop being such an ASSHOLE!" Rachael replied, nearly shouting her last word.

If Peter was offended by her words, he didn't show it. He merely winked at her and stayed focused as Kathy delivered the final directions.

Chapter Nine

GAME PLAY

Twister, as a family-friendly activity, is meant to be something that everyone can use to cut loose, burn energy, and, just in general, be silly. Twister at WCP Industries proved to be an entirely different entity. Hendrick and Kathy ran the game as if it was a CIA interrogation tactic. The questions were brutal, and each answer pushed the contestants into tighter, twisty-er positions. As it stood, Peter and Casey were pushed in such a way that their respective right and left shoulders were touching. The unwanted contact had Casey's face turning bright red- or it could be from the precarious positioning of Chaundra at that moment. Her backside was thrust upwards as she bent in a downward doggie pose, his leg placed between hers and his arms caged around her waist. Casey's mind wandered to just how close their bodies were. Intimately tangled together, despite or possibly because of the situation they were in, Casey could not fight the reaction of his body. She was a sweet temptation that pulled something primal out of him.

"Are we feeling the pressure yet?" Hendrick asked.

There were grunts and murmured replies from his employees.

"I think it's time to kick it up a notch." He grinned, though few could see a treacherous expression. "Kathy, spin the spinner, please."

Kathy flicked the spinner twice, collecting two color options.

"Have you ever confronted someone who was the cause of an intimate betrayal? If yes, right-hand blue. If no, left-hand yellow," Hendrick shouted gleefully.

Of course not. Casey thought as he moved his left hand further underneath Chaundra's body, grazing her right breast and collecting a teasing sensation of her stiffened nipple. He felt her shiver underneath him at the contact. He wanted, needed, the anger at Peter to rise up in this moment. Unfortunately, his body disagreed, and something else decided to rise to the occasion. He could feel Chaundra's body tense beneath him, and a sharp intake of breath tipped him off that she was picking up on every sensation his body was offering.

"Hey, Casey," Peter's taunting voice interrupted the moment. "Have you ever? Think you're man enough to tell the truth?"

Chapter Ten

LEFT ELBOW RED

Chaundra's mind replayed the scene in the hallway over and over. She barely registered the questions that Hendrick and Kathy were asking. She knew for sure that they were wildly inappropriate, but how could she focus on them when her lips and body were still tingling from Casey's kiss? It didn't help any that she was bent underneath him in the most precarious of positions. She felt hot all over, and the impulse to squirm her way out of the position was strong but not as strong as the pleasure she was taking from being so close to Casey. It didn't make any sense. She couldn't understand how she let herself get into this situation. She had never allowed herself to flirt at work, let alone kiss someone. However, every time they had a team building session, the lines between teamwork, professionalism, personal life, and attraction became more and more blurred. It didn't help that they spent time messaging each other between events regularly. Chaundra had begun to see the funny and creative side of Casey. He was a really interesting guy. Perhaps as interesting as the way his hand felt brushing against her breast or the steel that was firmly pressing into her backside. And that was the crux of the matter. She knew she should be turned off by the contact and, at the very least, offended. Instead, she welcomed it. That was it! She was going to draw a firm line in the sand after this event. No communication, nothing. Everything was getting out of hand and way too intense.

"... Think you're man enough to tell the truth?"

Peter's voice poked its way into her thoughts. Casey growled in response, but he didn't dignify Peter's comment with any further acknowledgment. She was proud of him. Now that her focus was fully back on the task at hand, she looked over her shoulder at Casey to give him a reassuring smile and a wink. The scowl on his face morphed into a dashingly handsome grin.

"If given the opportunity, would you make a move on someone else's partner? If yes- right-hand green. If no- left-hand red." Kathy's voice rang out.

What is the point of these questions? Chaundra thought. She knew these questions were extremely touchy. What did they have to do with building a team, she couldn't fathom.

"Already did, and she was worth the fun!" Peter laughed. "It was easy. *She* was easy."

Chaundra wanted to squeeze Casey's hand but they would have all collapsed in a heap if she moved.

"Asshole, Shut up!" Rachael said.

"What are you worried about, baby doll? She worked here but she's got nothing on you." Peter replied. "And the dude she was with was clearly a lose-"

Peter's words were cut off as Casey moved his left hand to red and took the opportunity to elbow Peter in the jaw.

"Ow! What the fuck, dude?!" Peter asked, moving his jaw from side to side.

"She may have been easy," Casey gritted out, "but she was my fiancé."

"Who are you talking about, bro?"

"Kerry. And I'm not your 'bro,' bro."

"Shit." Peter had the good sense to look mildly abashed. Then he looked down at Casey and smiled. "So you know just how good she was then. Sorry to poach one from you. You have good taste. Hey, Chaundra- Call me."

That was all it took. Suddenly the pretzel that they were all twisted in came apart as Casey stood abruptly up. Peter stumbled off to the side before regaining his footing.

"Leave Chaundra out of this," Casey said.

"What? Is she too good for sloppy seconds?" Peter replied as he stepped forward and shoved Casey's shoulder.

Casey responded by giving Peter a molly-wop of a slap across the face.

"You're too much of a bitch to waste a punch on. Show some respect. Don't you ever even mention Chaundra again. Don't let her name pass your lips. She's got nothing to do with this."

"I'm a bitch? You're the bitch who can't keep a woman," Peter said as he came forward and swung on Casey. Before she knew it, Casey and Peter were in a full-on brawl, fists flying.

"Gentleman!" Hendrick's amused voice cried out. "Gentleman, please! Pull yourselves together!"

Hendrick rushed over to the sparring men and passively attempted to intervene.

"This is a place of business. Take it outside, please!"

The brawlers were implacable. Having unleashed the anger and fury of his ex's betrayal, Casey could only see red. It was only Chaundra's touch that pulled some sense back into him, and he stepped back.

"No, seriously, outside boys. You clearly have some.... unresolved issues to work out." Hendrick giggled. "This exercise is all about problem-solving."

"You want to go? I'll beat the breaks off of your ass right now!" Peter said, his button-down shirt was torn open, and his jaw had begun to bruise.

"Screw you. You're not even worth the ride down the elevator. You're pathetic. You are NOTHING!" Casey said.

The room grew silent as Casey's words reverberated through the crowd of people. Never had a team building event seemed so divisive. Coming to blows seemed to be the opposite of what anyone running a business would want. However, it must be said. At that moment, everyone in the room was on the same page. Everyone agreed that Casey was well within his rights and because of his well-known actions, Peter really was pathetic. He spent all of his time at work peacocking, but it didn't stop him from being a douche. Perhaps Mr. Hendrick Pfeiffer was on to something- everyone was finally united in their opinions, surprisingly, even Peter.

Kathy cleared her throat and broke the silence.

"I think perhaps this is a good place to wrap things up. What do you say, Hendrick?"

"Indeed. I think you are right, Kathy. Everyone, thank you for coming out today. Go home and relax. I think we've achieved all that we need to today."

Everyone stood still, unsure of what to make of the situation.

"Shoo! Go home. The party's over," Mr. Hendrick said, turned to Kathy, and chuckled as they exited the room.

Chapter Eleven

INTERIM

Insta-chat *Travers:* Hey Chaundra! That was some team-building experience.

Insta-chat Jenkins: (Jenkins is typing...)

Insta-chat Jenkins: (Jenkins is typing...)

Insta-chat Travers: Is everything okay?

Insta-chat Jenkins: Hi Casey, Everything's fine.

Insta-chat Travers: I haven't heard from you. Want to meet up for coffee?

Insta-chat Jenkins: I don't think that's really a good idea.

Insta-chat Travers: Is it a bad time?

Insta-chat Jenkins: No. I just think we need to focus on our jobs. We're work colleagues. We should keep it that way.

Insta-chat Travers: It's just coffee *shrug emoji*

Insta-chat Travers: I thought we could work on *our* team building.

Insta-chat Jenkins: Listen, things... got out of hand. I don't want to talk about this at work. Let's just keep it professional. Thank you

END OF CHAT

Chaundra stared at her monitor, biting her lower lip in worry. Had she done the right thing? Casey was rapidly becoming more than just a person she had to do bi-monthly team-building objectives. She couldn't count the amount of times that her mind drifted to all of the moments their bodies touched. Worse, her mind replayed the kiss over and over. She hated how her body reacted at just the mention of his name. She despised how excited she became when his name popped up on her monitor to chat. That excitement was exactly how she knew that she had to distance herself from him. She didn't want to become another bit of WCP gossip. She wanted to succeed at this job and move up in the company. Being a workplace scandal was not going to get her there. Already, she saw the glances that she was getting from her colleagues who participated in the last Leadership Jam. They all heard the way Casey defended her name and saw the resulting fight. There was no way she could distance herself from all of that chatter. Soon, her direct reports and all of those who didn't attend would be gossiping like she and Casey were the latest tabloid couple. She just couldn't take it. Chaundra wanted to maintain a strong appearance, one without the taint of rumor. She had plans to ascend to the highest possible levels, whether here at WCP or possibly a future under her own corporation. No, she needed to keep her work life professional. It was bad enough that she had to fight to overcome all of the tales that were being told in her personal life. Family and so-called friends were building wilder and wilder tales about what had happened between her and Joel. She couldn't take it on both sides of her life. All of these thoughts went through her mind as she fought the urge to message Casey. No, she had done the right thing. This had to end. Everything between them had leaped beyond the bounds of professionalism.

Casey gripped his coffee mug tightly as he went to the break area. What had gone wrong? After the Twister episode, he felt confident that not only was he over the Kerry and Peter situation, but he was beyond ready to move on with Chaundra. Everything had felt so right. He was certain she was feeling the same thing. Was his understanding and discernment wrong, again? Self-doubt forced its way into his psyche once again.

Chapter Twelve

A CHAT WITH MABLE

HAVE A LITTLE HELP FROM OUR FRIENDS

Chaundra went home that evening feeling an uncomfortable tightness in her belly. She wanted to blame it on the toffee crunch iced mocha latte that she had at the company coffee shop, but she knew that wasn't really it. She needed someone to talk to about the way she had left things with Casey. Rachael was out of the question, though. First, she was too close to the situation. Chaundra already knew how Rachael felt. Secondly, this was Rachael's night to spend with her grandparents, one of whom was disabled. Her emotional distress wasn't a big enough deal to disrupt Rachael's family time.

Chaundra unlocked the door and walked into her freshly renovated and modernized mini-Brownstone-style house where the city meets the suburbs. She plopped her bags down on the hallway credenza, went to her kitchen, and pulled out a cocktail shaker, gin, limoncello, lemon juice, and a tall, thin Collins glass. Mixing cocktails always calmed her down and reminded her of the time she spent as a bartender in college when life was less complicated. With college on her mind, Chaundra sat down on her plush quilted wing-back chair in her living room, turned on some light jazz, picked up her phone, and sent a text. Her sweet girl, a gorgeous Afghan dog with flowing golden-brown fur, curled up by her feet. Even Lady Fiona knew she was out of sorts. If she couldn't talk to Rachael, why not reach out to one of her closest college friends?

Chaundra: Hi Mable

Mable: Hey Chaundra! How are you?

Chaundra: I'm fine... I have a huge favor to ask...

Mable: Let me guess, you need me to dog sit Lady Fiona for another team exercise?

Chaundra: Ack! You know me so well. I have another event coming up soon. I'm not sure how long it's going to be.

Mable: It's fine. I love that girl. So, what's up with the guy at work?

Chaundra: Nothing. What do you mean?

Mabel: Um...the party games? This kiss? Is that developing into something or what?

Chaundra: OMG! I should never have told you about that. I put an end to it

Mabel: Really? You seemed kinda into him...

Chaundra: Listen... I am a professional. I'm not going to feed the trolls at work

Mabel: No, I get that. Just, you kinda lit up when you were talking about him on Friday–I haven't seen you like that in forevers.

Chaundra: Can you talk now? This is too involved for a text

Mabel: Ya call me

"Hey, girl. How are you doing?" Chaundra asked when Mable picked up.

"I'm good–what about *you, girl,* coming off that highly inappropriate work event? Whooo! I know you like him!" Mable teased.

"What does like have to do with anything? I don't think I need drama right now. He's sweet and cute, and hot, and... you know what, it doesn't matter what he is. There's a lot of drama there. I told you about the fight, right?"

"Yes, that's *crazy,* but I like that he was kind of defending your honor–I know you don't need a defender, but hey, it's nice to see some chivalry in this day and age–I don't know, it seems like the chemistry is there–I know you work together, but you are kind of on equal level, right? You aren't each other's supervisors?"

"No, we're fine as far as working together is concerned. We don't even share a department. It's just you remember how weird everything got after Joel? None of our friends could stop talking about it or looking at me "that way."

"Ug. Joel. I'm sorry, but I'm still mad at him...I shouldn't be, but I am." Chaundra could hear the irritation in Mable's voice.

"Me too. I don't want to be, but I am. I'm not in love with him, but everything that came after is still with me. What if Casey isn't what he seems? What if we become the talk of the office and things go bad? Everyone will be giving me those looks again. I can't do that at home and at work.. It's just too much." Chaundra took a large sip of her Tom Collins, trying to wash down her doubt.

"Ok, but can't you keep it down low? I know you're good at keeping secrets–you're in different departments, so you probably don't interact at work that much. I mean, even if he's not the ONE, you just need to blow off some steam, girl. He can be your palette cleanser. It can be a fun rebound! You need to do something for yourself.

"He would be a delicious amuse bouche," Chaundra giggled.

"Haaa! Now you're talking! Mouth-watering! You gotta jump on this!"

"Maybe you're right, but what am I going to do now? I totally cold-shouldered him today when he asked for coffee. I'm scared for the next team build.

"Does Rachael know about all this?"

"No, not yet. You know how she is. If she got her teeth into this situation.... How could I possibly escape?"

Mabel laughed heartily. "So true! Does she think he's a good person? Does she like him?"

"She does like him. She was the first to point out how cute he was. Plus, she thought the fight was super hot. I know she's low-key "shipping" us. Ughh...." Chaundra flopped down on her bed like a frustrated teenager. "Why are boys so difficult?"

"I know...boys...but honestly, Rachael has good taste, and I know you are discerning, so if you are feeling this guy, you should just go for it! What's the worst that can happen?"

"I don't know... that I like him, he likes me. "

"Oh. You're afraid it actually *will* work out..."

"Maybe.' Chaundra sighed. "The thing is that I do want a relationship. I want all of the good things. I thought I already had that. I don't know if my heart can take it."

"No, I get that. But you can't stay on the sidelines forever, Chaundra. It's not that often a really good man comes along, so you have to put your foot in the water. That's my humble opinion. It's been almost a year. I know celibacy ain't easy–I'm living the dry spell over here..."

"Celibacy and pimpin'... who knew they had so much in common." Chaundra laughed.

Mabel laughed raucously. "But you get what I'm saying, right?"

"I do. I" 'm sure you could end your dry spell," Chaundra said pointedly. "You just need to figure out how to break down a brick wall. I'm just saying. Maybe we both need a little boldness."

"I mean, *yeeeees* but...I'm not as free as you are to *fraternize*...It's not that I'm not *interested*, but I really, really can't go there." Mable pointed out reluctantly.

"Maybe, maybe not. So are you saying you'll live through me?"

"Will I get a vicarious thrill from you? Yes! But that's not my main reason for saying this! I just want you to move on. I want you to believe you can be happy. It actually can work out! "

"Thanks, Mabes. I appreciate you. I'll try to find my happy."

Chapter Thirteen

BASKETBALL

The last squeak of sneakers and bouncing balls followed the guys as they walked to the locker room. Casey's head dipped slightly in defeat.

"Way to miss that free throw, man," Jacobson wheezed.

"Yeah, you were off your game tonight. We shoulda killed them," Brick chimed in.

"I bet I know. You're too busy thinking about that chick. Get your head outta them panties and into the game." Jacobson slapped Casey on the shoulder.

"Who's panties you into, Casey?" Brick smirked

"Nobody's panties. Jacobson is just fantasizing. Are you having daytime wet dreams about me? I didn't know you were interested," Casey said, glowering at Jacobson.

"Oh, please. You forget that I see you at work. I see those puppy dog eyes whenever she walks by with that thick, round ass."

"Fuck you, man!" Casey shoved the smaller man back a few steps. "Don't be talking about her like that."

"I thought there *was* nobody..."

"Whatever, man. Don't be such a pussy about it." Jacobson said and turned to Brick. "Casey totally has a crush on his teambuilding partner. The lovely Chaundra Jenkins."

"Wait, what? I know Chaundra! We're dog park friends! She's a really cool person, also a beautiful woman. See, that's how you describe a female, Jacobson. Are you seeing her?" Brick asked, his eyes wide.

Casey sighed and sat down on the bench in front of his locker.

"Nah, man, we're not dating. I thought we might be something, but she's totally icing me. Says she wants to be professional." Casey ran his fingers through his curls in frustration.

"Ah, sorry, that's too bad. Tough when you work together."

"Right. And it's talk like that," Casey turned and poked Jacobson in the chest. "That's preventing her from even considering me. She doesn't want to be WCP News."

"I fucking hate gossip. It reminds me of middle school." Brick said, shaking his head. "But I guess your loss is another man's gain?" Now Brick shrugged.

Casey looked up at Brick and fought to hold back a feral growl. Chaundra was not meant for another man's gain. He could feel it in his bones. It was becoming clearer than ever that he needed to try to get through to Chaundra as soon as he could. What if Brick was trying to be that other man? There would be no obstacle, and he seemed like the perfect non-toxic type of guy that a woman like Chaundra would love.

"I didn't say it was a total loss. I'm not giving up yet. I just have to get some facetime with her. We have a way of understanding each other."

"Right on!" Jacobson cheered, "See, I had to talk about that fat ass and curvy body to get you back in the saddle. Now you're manning up."

"I swear to.... One more word, and you're going to be wearing that grin while staring at the ceiling."

"I'ma hold you down while Casey hits you. You are cro-magnon. I don't care if you're a good point guard..." Brick said, punching Jacobson in his bicep. Jacobson just laughed, and Brick turned back to Casey, patting him on the shoulder. "But good luck with that, man. She's worth it."

"She is," Casey said simply.

"Beer?" Jacobson asked, grabbing his bag and heading to the door.

"I've seen and heard enough from your troglodyte brain. Tomorrow morning is soon enough for me. I'm out," Casey replied.

"I've got a lot going on at work. I need to prepare some things. I'll catch you guys next week, maybe. Hopefully, Casey's back on his *game*." Brick said, then waved and walked out.

"Cool man, see you next week," Jacobson yelled after Brick. He was a few steps behind Brick when he stopped and turned back to Casey. "In all seriousness, I had to get you fired up. Trust me. Now, go get your girl." Jacobson gave a small jump and fist pumped the air.

"What do you think this is a 1980s teen movie? Get outta here." Casey tossed his sweat-soaked towel towards Jacobson's face.

Jacobson just laughed and made a kissy face at Casey and then walked out of the locker room, leaving Casey to sit and consider his next plan of action. He couldn't wait for the next event.

From: Kathy Starnes (on behalf of Hendrick Pfeiffer, CEO)

To: WCP Department Lead Distribution List

Subject: Quarterly Leadership Jam (Session Three Update)

Dear Colleagues,

After the tremendous success of our last Leadership Jam, our next session is going to be extra special. Please come prepared with the essentials for a weekend getaway. This weekend will be all about connection, vulnerability, and willingness to expose ourselves on another level.

Please be prompt and ready to leave at 2:00 P.M. this Friday afternoon. Sunscreen and toiletries will be provided.

Sincerely,

Hendrick Pfeiffer, CEO

WCP Industries

Chapter Fourteen

THE PARKING LOT

"Girl, come on! What is going on with you?" Rachael asked.

"Nothing. I'm fine," Chaundra replied. The two women stood with their weekender bags at their feet. Chaundra fidgeted with the strap of her bag, picking at the stitching. She picked at it so much that the fibers were starting to show wear and beginning to fray.

"You can't seriously expect me to believe that. You haven't been right since the last team build. Was it the fight? I know something was going on with you and Casey even before things got ugly."

"I have no idea what you're talking about."

"Right. You're perfectly fine," Rachael deadpanned. "So, do you always stand around destroying your very expensive luggage?" Rachael looked pointedly at Chaundra's hands.

"Okay, fine. I might be a little nervous to see Casey again. Some things happened last time."

"Oh really?" Rachael said, tilting her head to the side. "Do tell me more. I knew by the way you were looking at each other that something was up."

"We, um, we kind of kissed." Chaundra blushed. "But it will never happen again. It was extremely unprofessional, and I'm embarrassed to even admit it."

"Ohh, I knew it!! Don't be embarrassed. Shoot, I'm jealous. Casey is gorgeous and actually a decent guy. Why couldn't I get paired with someone extremely kissable? So what was it like? Did it come out of nowhere? I can't believe a quiet guy like him made a first move like that." Rachael prattled on.

"Well, technically, that wasn't our first contact." Chaundra winced.

"Are you kidding me? How did I not know any of this?" Rachael shouted.

"Shh.... I don't want anyone to know."

"Not even me, apparently," Rachael huffed. "Well, you better spill it all now. I'm not going to give you a break until I know it all. And here I always thought I would be the one with a scandalous and torrid workplace romance."

"Fine, I'll tell you if it will keep you from getting any louder. And it is NOT a romance!"

"You better!"

"At our first jam session, I somehow ended up sitting in his lap and then we fell asleep in separate sleeping bags but woke up spooning the next morning. And then, last time, he was so upset by your partner. I just wanted to comfort him when he walked out of the session. I can't explain it. One minute we're bonding over shared rejection, and the next minute, we were sharing the kiss to end all kisses. Like, I felt that kiss in my hair follicles. It was so thorough!"

"It was that good? I want to be kissed like that by a fine-ass man like Casey."

"Well, it's not going to happen again. That much I know."

"Why not? You obviously like each other, and you're both single. What's the problem?"

"The problem is that we're colleagues. I can't keep kissing at work! It's not appropriate. I want to be taken seriously, and this is not the way to do it. I told Casey that we need to keep things strictly business."

Rachael stared at Chaundra before lightly smacking her on the arm.

"Are you for real? Don't miss a good thing just because you're scared. I think you're using work as an excuse. What are you really afraid of?"

"Oh, I don't know, getting caught and becoming fodder for the company rumor mill. I think that's more than enough."

"Uh-uh. Nope. I'm not falling for that one. Try again. Did you feel a real connection with him?"

"Yes, but that's not the point-"

"Actually, that is the point. That's what you're afraid of. Not everyone is Joel."

Chaundra started to say more, but she noticed that Casey was heading their way with a big smile.

"Hi, Casey! We're over here." Rachael called to him.

Chaundra gave Rachael a look, which she ignored.

"Hi, Rachael. Chaundra, can I talk to you for a second?"

"I don't want to be a third wheel. I think you two have plenty to talk about," Rachael said and walked away toward another group of waiting employees.

"Hi, Case, what's on your mind?"

"Is everything okay with us? I know you said you want to keep things professional, and I respect that, but I thought we were at least becoming work friends. I feel like you're freezing me out."

"I'm not freezing you out. It's just that I think we get confused and lose our focus when we spend too much time alone together. I'm refocusing us."

"Refocus. Got it." Casey nodded. "The thing is, you're practically the only thing I can focus on right now. I've been worried that I offended you or that I pushed things too far. Did I?"

"No, nothing like that." Chaundra looked around, hoping for an escape. Where was Mr. Pfeiffer when you needed him? He was always good for an ill-timed interruption. Now, when she needed him, he was nowhere to be found.

"You didn't offend me. I just... things are happening too fast. I figured if we spend less time alone, we can keep our ducks in a row."

Casey looked at her, searching her face for what she was leaving out. Chaundra looked everywhere and anywhere to avoid his gaze.

"Listen, Casey, I don't think I'm ready to be the subject of office gossip right now."

"We don't have to be. What you and I do, what we feel, that's between you and me alone."

Chaundra shook her head and took a step back.

"This is all too soon after the whole Joel thing. I just... I can't." Taking a deep breath, she continued, "We need to cool off before we get too hot and burn. You said we're work friends. Let's just keep it that way."

Before Casey could refute what Chaundra had said, finally, Mr. Hendrick interrupted the cacophony of voices in the parking lot.

"WCP Leaders! Before we board the buses, I want to let you know that we are all in for a real treat! I have the most amazing accommodations set up for this weekend. I hope you are prepared to let go of all your work stress, enjoy the tropical surf and sand, and bond! After the intensity of our previous events, this is a time to let loose and party! Alright now, folks... All Aboard!" He raised his arms in a grand come here motion and began ushering his employees onto the bus.

"Chaundra..."

"Casey. Let's just leave it for now. We need to get on the bus."

"Ok, but I really think we need to talk," Casey said.

"We will. I promise."

Chapter Fifteen

FUN IN THE SUN

The teambuilders were all abuzz as they stepped off the airport shuttles and took in their first view of Playa del Hendrick. Of course, Mr. Pfeiffer would have a private island named after him, and of course, it would be breathtakingly beautiful. Clearly, he did nothing by half-measures.

"Welcome to my little slice of paradise. Please see Ms. Starnes for your room assignments."

Mr. Hendrick Pfeiffer gazed over the group with a swelling of joy in his heart. He felt as if each and every one of them were his children. Everything was coming together for his babies in a way that was even better than he had originally planned. Real connections were being made, even if somewhat reluctantly. Here and there, he saw little signs of resistance to his plans, but he was confident that he could tweak things in his favor. He sighed in satisfaction. Everything was going to be as it should be.

Casey and Chaundra stood in line, feeling the electricity flowing between them and adamantly ignoring it. Casey had spent all of their travel time trying to understand what had gone wrong and attempting to tamp down his growing attraction and feelings. He only hoped that once he could get some distance from her, he would be able to put things into perspective.

"Great!" Kathy's brisk voice penetrated Casey's thoughts. "You're together. Here is your room assignment and your keys."

She handed Casey a packet of information and gave Chaundra two card keys.

"Now, off you go! Can't stand here all day. Others are waiting." Kathy shooed them along.

"Which key is mine?" Casey asked.

"I'm not sure. They both have the same symbol on them but no numbers. Check the info packet. Maybe that will clear things up," Chaundra replied.

"It just has a map. Looks like our destination matches the symbol on the keys," Casey said as he looked over the map.

Silently, they began to walk, following the trail outlined on their map. They were surrounded by the fragrance of tropical flowers, the breeze of the ocean tickling their skin. Birdsong serenaded them as they wandered further into the compound. Their journey came to an abrupt end as they faced a small bungalow. On the front door was a symbol that matched their key.

"Well, this is odd," Chaundra said as she looked around and realized that they were fairly isolated on the path. They hadn't passed any other cottages for several minutes. "Kind of isolated, don't you think?"

"It is, but I think we're in the right place. Let's try one of the keys. Maybe there's a second apartment on the other side of the cottage." He took his key and opened the door. "Looks like mine works, not that I'm claiming this half. Let's check it out and then see about the other space."

Little did they know, Mr. Hendrick Pfeiffer was no longer playing games. There would be no second abode. Just one big communal living space- a large king-size bed sat center stage in the room with a gauzy, mosquito net-style canopy draped around it. Pillar candles decorated the space. Large cushions were scattered around the room to add extra seating. A modern state-of-the-art kitchenette took up one corner of the space, while a small seating area resided in the opposite corner. Behind the bed was a breathtaking view of a lanai that led to a private pool/beach area. The only other doorways led to a bathroom/closet area and a laundry facility.

"We have to go back. Clearly, a mistake has been made," Chaundra said, voice almost frantic. She knew that she could not stay here. It screamed romance. Plus, there were two of them... where was the second sleeping area??

Leaving their bags behind, they made a speedy retreat back to find Kathy and get everything sorted out.

"Kathy! Kathy!" Chaundra called out. "There's been a mistake!"

Seated on a rock in an apparent moment of tranquility, Kathy Starnes sat with her eyes closed. Her expression was one of peace, although if one looked closely, there was a bit of strain and tension in the way she held her eyebrows. Her hold on peace was tenuous at best.

"Ms. Starnes," Casey addressed her more calmly. "I'm sorry to interrupt you, but there seems to have been a mistake with the accommodations."

Kathy inhaled deeply, the frown lines about her lips becoming pronounced.

"What sort of mistake?" Each one of her words came out in hard, brittle pronunciation. "I rarely make mistakes, Mr. Travers."

"It's just that Chaundra and I have been assigned to the same space."

"Every team has been paired in a shared bungalow." Her eyes glowered over the top of her Ray Bans. Her stare threatened to turn Casey to stone.

"In a one-bedroom bungalow, though?" Chaundra asked. She was not one to be cowed so quickly by a simple look.

"Hmm. I see." Kathy looked both Casey and Chaundra in the eye for a moment before dismissively pushing up her sunglasses. "I can't do anything about that at the moment. If you had thoroughly read your packet rather than frowning at your luxury accommodations, you would know that we have a soiree on the beach in about 45 minutes. You will barely have time to get yourselves changed and ready. I will have your situation sorted out before the end of the night. Now hurry back and get ready. Thank you, Miss Jenkins. Mr. Travers."

With not even a glance back in their direction, Kathy stood and sauntered down the beach path in the opposite direction of their cabin.

Casey and Chaundra stood in shock at their dismissal until Kathy disappeared around the bend and was lost to the tall, sweet grasses that favored sandy ground.

"Well, ain't that about a bitch?" Chaundra grumbled. "Did she, did she just walk away from us?"

"She did. I believe we have been dismissed. Let's head back and get ready for this beach party. I'm sure everything will be sorted before night's end." Casey said. Indeed, it would be.

Chapter Sixteen

THE BUNGALOW

Casey and Chaundra entered the bungalow to an unexpected site. Placed upon the bed were two packages, bedazzled with their names in rhinestone. Casey raised his eyebrow and nodded his head toward the bed.

"Ladies first," he said.

"Really, Casey?"

Chaundra wanted to act reluctant but the reality is that she loved opening presents. Rushing over to the bed, she grabbed the box and shook it. She heard a soft woosh and a slight thud.

"Whatever it is, it's fairly insubstantial," she said. "Oh, and there's a little card!"

Dear Chaundra,

I hope you don't mind, but I took the liberty of picking out a little something for everyone to wear to the beach party. I hope you like it!

Remember, we're building something special here. Please be on the sand at 7:30 P.M. sharp.

Your Friendly CEO,

Hendrick Pfeiffer

"I guess we all have a uniform to wear. Open yours with me,"

Chaundra patted the space next to her on the bed. Casey joined her, and they began to rip away the packaging. Casey was the first to get his open. He stared in consternation, not really sure what he was seeing.

"What in the world?" Chaundra exclaimed as she shook out her "gift." In her hands was a flimsy contraption of strings and swatches of fabric. "Case, show me what you've got."

"I'm almost too embarrassed ... here." He handed it over to her. In her hands was a skimpy, high-cut, speedo swimsuit made of *very* thin fabric. Stuck to the wrapping paper was another stringy contraption that might have been a shirt or a shredded rag. It was really hard to tell. Chaundra cackled with laughter.

"At least I'm not the only one. Here." She handed him her bits of fabric. He held up one of the skimpiest bikinis he had ever seen.

"I know I've said this before, but what is going on with these team-building events? They just seem to get more and more.... out there."

"I'm beginning to think we *shouldn't* think at all. Just go with the flow. At least there will be other people in the same position as us." Chaundra giggled.

"I guess. But if this turns into some weird sex orgy... We're outta there."

"Oh, one hundred percent!"

Casey went to the laundry room, and Chaundra went to change in the bathroom. When they came out, it took everything for Casey to look Chaundra in the eye and not let his eyes feast on her curves. She was petite and voluptuous in a way that made him want to sink his teeth into her luscious body. For her part, Chaundra briefly let her eyes wander over the planes of Casey's body. His broad shoulders and muscled chest made her want to reach out and touch somebody. Casey's body to be precise. She quickly looked up at his face and gave him a coy smile.

"I suppose we should get going."

"Yeah."

They continued to smile at each other, not moving. The only thing that interrupted them was the sudden buzzing of an insect.

"Did that man pack any bug repellent for us? He's got everything else planned out."

"Who knows? Anything is possible at this point. Let's get going, Chaundie," Casey grinned as he tried out the new nickname.

"Okay, Casey Case." Chaundra walked out the door first, giving a pleasing view of her backside and the delightful bounce of her butt cheeks. He was in heaven and hell all at the same time.

Chapter Seventeen

BEACH PARTY

Before they even arrived at the beachfront, they could hear the sounds of laughter and soft Jack Johnson-style beach music. Tiki torches guided them toward the party, and the added aroma of roasting food and coconut made for an enticing aroma. Once on the beach, they were greeted by their coworkers in various beach attire that ranged from skimpy to just shy of modest. Everyone seemed perfectly comfortable despite the fact that no one had planned on being surrounded by their coworkers on the beach. Some had cocktails, and others had marshmallows on skewers roasting over the fire pits. Surprisingly, everyone seemed comfortable. Casey and Chaundra looked at each other and shrugged.

"Maybe we were worried for nothing. Other than a questionable swimsuit here and there, everything seems above board for once." Casey said.

They started to mingle and relax, and then the giggle began.

Both tensed as they felt the heat of another body close behind them. Then, the clasp of a strong, heavy hand landed on each of their shoulders.

"You two look good enough to eat!" Hendrick said and then

laughed boisterously. "Kidding. But seriously. I'm so glad you're here. You know, seeing each other in one of your most vulnerable states is really what this is all about. How can you not form a bond with a bunch of people that you have frolicked nearly naked on the beach? And don't you two worry. I lead by example. See?"

They could hear the grin in his voice but were reluctant to turn around.

"Oh come, come now. Don't be shy. You've shown me yours. It's only fair that I show you mine."

Casey and Chaundra turned around to take in the glory that was Mr. Hendrick Pfeiffer. Standing proudly before them was a hairy man with a keg rather than a pot belly. Unwantingly, they perused the bear of a man's body and discovered that he had been exceedingly kind to the rest of the men on this excursion. Kind because he did not expect anyone to be clad in the same suit as himself.

"Pretty fetching, isn't it? Designer. They call it a mankini. I love it!"

It was hideous. Chaundra had to gulp in air to hold back her immediate sense of revulsion. It could hardly be called a swimsuit. It was more like a testicle slingshot. In bright neon green, trimmed in bubble gum pink, was a small strip of fabric that enclosed Hendrick's privates and wrapped around one hip, almost pulling all of his bits to one side. Perhaps it wouldn't have been so disturbing had he been waxed or clean-shaven, but that was not the case.

Casey was speechless. He attempted to clear his throat and speak up, but he just couldn't do it.

"Well, I won't keep you two luh-, ahem, I won't keep you two. I hope you've limbered up. We're about to do a limbo contest! How low can you go? Heeheheheeheheh!" Hendrick laughed and trotted off, giving them a view of his tiny white cheeks practically glowing in the firelight.

"Now, that is not something you don't see every day," Casey said.

"Nor is it something you want to see. My eyes need to be bleached," Chaundra said.

Just then, a shrill whistle pierced through the sounds of the festivities. All eyes turned toward the largest bonfire. Next to it, standing on a bamboo and grass stage, stood Kathy Starnes decked out in a leopard bikini, hair pulled back and secured by what almost looked like a small bone. Hendrick lurked behind her, appearing as a sumo wrestler bodyguard with a severe wardrobe malfunction.

"Attention up here, folks! We're very glad that you're having a good time, but we can't forget our original purpose for being here. What's our purpose?" Kathy's strident voice called out.

Silence met her as everyone looked around, unsure how to respond.

"Come on, people... When I say team, you say building. Team!"

"Building!" everyone murmured.

"We can do better than that! TEAM!!"

"BUILDING!"

"Again! TEAM!!" Kathy shouted and punctuated it by doing a herkie, bringing out her inner cheerleader. The crowd went wild. Cheers went up all around, screaming Team Building and Kathy's name.

"Well, that was unexpected!" Chaundra said, nudging Casey. "I never would have pictured Kathy as a cheerleader."

"Stranger things.... tonight is a night of very strange things," Casey replied.

Without realizing it, Casey and Chaundra once again stood close together. Their arms brushed lightly against each other, fingers teasing to be intertwined.

"My, my, my... aren't you two a cozy treat to see." Rachael sidled up next to the pair.

"Rachael! What's up!" Chaundra ignored the intent of Rachael's comment. "This is crazy, right?"

"It sure is. Where do they have you staying? I tried to find you in the complex after I unpacked, but you were nowhere to be found."

"We're down the trail in that direction. Way at the end. There was some mistake with our rooms. Kathy is supposed to be sorting it out," Casey replied.

"Hey, Casey," Rachael replied. "What sort of mistake?"

Casey blushed. "They have us in what looks like a honeymoon cottage. There's only one room."

Rachael looked at Chaundra and raised her eyebrows.

"That's so interesting. You know you're also staying in the complete opposite direction of everyone else. Everyone is staying in the complex in this little building with mini-suites. Everyone has their own. I don't think there are any singles left."

"What?" Chaundra asked. That didn't match what Kathy had described. Her stomach started flip-flopping nervously.

"Yeah, I knocked on every door, and each one was occupied," Rachael said. "I guess you two will just have to figure.... something out." She gave them a lopsided grin and sauntered away.

This cannot be happening. Chaundra thought. Her worry replaced the amusement that she had from watching Kathy's antics. Was the universe and WCP conspiring against her? All she wanted to do was get through this weekend and not cross any more lines with Casey. She shivered slightly as a breeze wafted through the crowd.

"Feeling cold?" he whispered into her ear so that he could be heard over the crowd. She shook her head no, but the heat of his breath made her shiver even more. "You look like you're freezing. Here."

Casey pulled her close and wrapped his arm around her shoulder. "Better?"

"Yes," Chaundra whispered. She didn't want his touch to feel so good, but damn if it didn't hit the spot. She felt all sorts of heat run through her body.

"We love that team spirit!" Kathy shouted into the microphone. The Limbo music started to play. "Time for our first team event. The Limbo!!!"

Chapter Eighteen

HOW LOW CAN YOU GO

Everyone assembled in front of the stage as the instrumental version of *The Limbo* continued to play. Rachael and Peter were selected to hold the bar. Casey was distracted from the action ahead of him as his mind pondered Rachael's words from earlier. There were no more rooms left? If that were true, wouldn't Kathy have known that when they approached her earlier? Rachael had to be mistaken, not that he didn't love the idea of more alone time with Chaundra. Even now, standing in line for this ridiculous dance from the 50s, he could feel waves of tension and attraction flow between them. He understood why Chaundra had felt like she needed to distance herself from him in a practical way. He just couldn't convince his body and soul that it was the right thing to do. Somehow, he was going to win her over. This connection was unlike anything he had felt before, and he was compelled to make it permanent.

"...As you all know, we at WCP like to do things a little bit differently from everyone else. For this to be a team building experience, you will be limbo-ing with your partners. If one of you can't make it through, then you are both out. So you'll have to get creative if you want to make it as the last couple standing." Mr. Pfeiffer delivered the instructions to the group. "And just to sweeten the pot, this challenge has a prize if you win. The team that wins will receive two bonus vacation days in addition to their already allotted supply!"

Excitement rippled through the crowd. Two extra days off with pay was worth joining up for.

"The first team to drop out will replace our bar holders so that they can compete. Now, don't you folks worry. I don't expect you to do this on your own. Kathy and I will participate as a team as well!"

Kathy shot Hendrick a surprised look and briefly grimaced but then corrected her expression. He returned her look with a cheese-eating grin.

"Everyone, let's begin!" Kathy shouted.

The first couple of rounds went smoothly. By the fourth round, the bar had dropped to just below chest level, and several teams had to drop out because one or more of them just did not have the flexibility to get through. Peter and Rachael joined the competition and were doing surprisingly well. By the eighth round, only three couples remained- Casey and Chaundra, Peter and Rachael, and surprisingly, Mr. Pfeiffer and Ms. Starnes.

Casey, Chaundra, Rachael, and Peter stood on the sidelines watching.

"Who knew those two were so flexible?" Rachael asked.

"Honestly, I wish they were less so. I'm seriously afraid for that mankini. If he bends backward any further, I don't know how it's going to stay on," Chaundra said.

"I guess it's high quality. They just made it through again. Our turn, dollface." Peter said and grabbed Rachael's hand.

"You know we're totally going to win this, right?" Casey said.

"Oh yeah, we've got this in the bag."

Just then, Peter slipped and fell under the bar, pulling Rachael down with him. Rachael gave him a dirty look as they walked off, disqualified.

"And then there were two!" Hendrick shouted gleefully, urging Casey and Chaundra along.

Hands on each other's backs for support, Casey and Chaundra danced up to the bar and made it through for one more round. It was now down to Kathy and Hendrick. The crowd was rooting for Casey and Chaundra. After all, what would Mr. Pfeiffer do with additional PTO? It would be nice for Kathy but even better for a co-worker like them. As they approached the bar, it was clear Kathy's flexibility was stellar she was going to slide through with ease. It was more unclear for Hendrick. He spread his legs wide, leaned back, and humped at the air to pull himself through. His motion was all the more disconcerting due to the nature of his swimsuit. While there was the threat of a malfunction earlier in the competition, at this point, the malfunction was imminent. The stars, the moon, and the flickering torchlight all came together in that moment to spotlight Hendrick. The teambuilders held their breaths. Some looked away in fear, others laughed or coughed nervously, and for the unfortunate few- they were transfixed. Eyes focused on that teeny weenie mankini. Two things happened at once, Hendrick bumped the bar on his final upward thrust, and his right testicle fled the scene of his mankini. Chaundra was amongst those who couldn't look away. She was there to bear witness to a surprisingly hairy, wrinkled testicle. Quickly, she turned her head away and pressed her face into Casey's chest. Instinctively, his arms wrapped around her.

"Please tell me I did not see what I think I saw."

"I wish I could. We have now seen more of our boss than any employee should ever have to see."

"Heheheh! Excuse me, everyone, I seem to have had a little accident. Let's all congratulate our winners! Come on up to the stage, Casey and Chaundra!" Hendrick said as he readjusted his swimsuit and walked up to the stage. Reluctantly, they joined him on the stage.

"Let's hear it for Casey and Chaundra! What are you two going to do with your extra time off?"

"Um.... no idea, but I know I'll make the most of it," Casey said. The crowd laughed and applauded.

"Be sure that you do! Everyone feel free to mingle and grab some food. There's a buffet setup behind the stage," Hendrick said and sent everyone on their way.

"Now, let's all get together for a photo op." He spread his arms wide and wrapped one around Casey and attempted to pull Chaundra in on the other side.

"Oh, I don't think I should get that close to you, sir. I haven't been feeling too well. I wouldn't want to get you sick," Chaundra replied. Hendrick had not sanitized his hands after touching his scrotum, and the thought of touching him was giving her the ick.

"Well, let's hurry and get this picture taken," Hendrick said. The photo was quickly taken. "So you say you're not feeling well? We can't have you around the other leaders. I'm afraid I'm quarantining you to your quarters for the next couple of days. Since you've been glued at the hip, Casey, you're quarantined as well."

Chaundra's eyes went wide.

"You can't be serious, sir. I'll be fine. Plus, there's been a mistake. We're stuck in the same cabin. Kathy was going to change it."

"I'm sorry. We can't worry about that now. For everyone's health, it's better that you ride this out together. By the time you both feel better, I'm sure we'll have your accommodations all sorted. Off you go!"

"But-" Casey started.

"Say no more. As it is, you may have infected everyone. Run along! Kathy or myself will be in touch to see if you need anything. Get better!"

There was nothing more that Casey or Chaundra could say. Mr. Hendrick Pfeiffer had spoken.

Hendrick feigned a look of concern as he watched them walk back down the path towards their isolated cabin.

"Should I work on finding a second accommodation? I've already made the other arrangements that you had planned," Kathy asked from his side.

"To what end? No, I think they'll be just fine."

That damned giggle followed Casey and Chaundra all the way to the cabin.

Chapter Nineteen

QUARANTINE!

"Are you really sick?" Casey asked.

"No, I just wanted to avoid touching his testicle hands."

Casey cracked up.

"Testicle hands? Ha! I guess you're right."

"I just didn't expect that he'd ban us both from the rest of the event for two days. I'm sorry, Case." Chaundra was contrite.

"It's okay. I can think of worse company." Casey gave her a lopsided grin. She returned the smile.

"Me too. So how do you want to do this?"

Chaundra pulled out her key and opened the bungalow door. The scent of roses was the first indication that things were not as they had left them. Next, the flickering candlelight caught Chaundra's eye.

"Yo, what is going on? We're in the right place, aren't we?" Chaundra asked Casey after they had both fully entered the space.

"The key worked, so we have to be."

The kitchenette table had a silver bucket filled with ice, an open bottle of white wine, and a bottle of champagne nestled inside. Silver-covered dinner plates were placed at each seat of the table.

"No, this is definitely for us. Look, there's a card on the table with our names." Chaundra wandered over to the table and picked up the card. Casey came to her side and read the card over her shoulder.

From: Kathy Starnes (on behalf of Hendrick Pfeiffer, CEO)

To: WCP Department Lead Distribution List

Subject: Quarterly Leadership Jam (Session Three Update) Re: Casey Travers and Chaundra Jenkins

"How did we become the subject of a memo?" Chaundra asked.

"Beats me!" Casey said and continued to read the card aloud.

Dear Colleagues,

It has come to my attention that both Casey Travers and Chaundra Jenkins have spent several months working on their team-building skills. In light of their success and the strength of their burgeoning relationship, I wanted to bestow upon you both my sincerest blessing and joy at the unity you have both created.

I am aware that the last year has been extremely trying on an emotional level for both of you. At times, we believe that we have found the perfect teammate, but for whatever reason, we are wrong. Third-party intervention is necessary. I hope you don't mind that I have taken it upon myself to sort things out for you. Trust yourselves, trust your hearts. Team C+C is stronger and better together... in all and every way.

Sincerely yours,

Hendrick Pfeiffer, CEO

P.S. The sheets are satin! Enjoy!

Silence filled the bungalow except for the romantic lo-fi R&B that played from hidden speakers.

"What-" Chaundra wanted to say something but was at a complete loss for words.

"I don't- You know what, let's ignore this and take the lids off of these plates. I'm starving, how about you?" Casey asked.

"Famished. If nothing else, I won't turn down free champagne."

They sat down at their respective seats and removed the lids from their trays. A veritable surf and turf feast lay before them. The delectable aroma of filet mignon topped with fresh lump crabmeat, broiled lobster, and shrimp excited their palates. Glasses of wine were poured, and they began to eat. Chaundra picked up a shrimp and placed it delicately between her lips. A soft moan escaped her lips. Casey couldn't keep his eyes off of her perfect, plump lips. He knew that the food was delicious but couldn't touch the flavor of her kisses. He thought he was hungry but realized his hunger had nothing to do with the spread that lay before him. The pleasure sounds that she made as she tasted that first bite drove him crazy. He took a long pull from his glass of wine, hoping to refocus.

"This food is really good," Chaundra said.

"That memo was something else," Casey's words came on top of Chaundra's.

"Right? I don't know what he was talking about," Chaundra watched as Casey drank more wine. The bob of his Adam's apple tantalized her. She briefly imagined peppering his neck with kisses and flicks of her tongue. Suddenly, she was very thirsty, too.

"And that part about satin sheets... Craziness! It's like he wants us to believe all of these events have been created just to draw us together. Like, really?" Casey asked. His eyebrow quirked in disbelief.

Damn, this man is fine!!! Chaundra thought. Quickly, she put a piece of the filet in her mouth.

"I know. It's just ridiculous," she said, chewing the tender meat. "That's just not possible. It's almost like he's telling us we should be making love instead of eating."

"Shouldn't we?" Casey's eyes went wide. He hadn't meant to say the quiet part out loud.

"What?" Chaundra asked.

"I just meant, shouldn't we go outside and check out the pool after we finish eating? I bet we can see the stars. That's what I meant," Casey tried to cover his tracks.

"Oh, yes, that's a great idea." *This is a terrible idea.* Chaundra thought. Can it get more romantic than moonlight, a tropical paradise, and sparkling water?

They finished their meal in somewhat awkward and heavily charged silence.

"Shall we go outside?" Casey asked.

Chapter Twenty

BY THE LIGHT OF THE MOON

Once outside, the romance of the moment seemed to escalate. The moon was large and full. Every star shined like a jewel. The fragrance of wildflowers perfumed the air. The pool glowed with floating candles, and a dish of chocolate-covered strawberries floated on a tray in the water.

"This is breathtaking," Chaundra said.

Casey turned to look at her. He had spent so much time resisting his own desires that he could barely stand it. Her velvet skin looked caressable and soft. He longed to touch her. Any part of her skin would satiate his hunger. Even the shell of her ear was tantalizing. He could almost feel his tongue gliding across it, then trailing kisses down her neck until he reached her neckline, his kisses and tongue darting further until he could suckle at her firm, taut...

"Let's go swimming!" he said abruptly and jumped into the pool.

Chaundra laughed. "Boy, you're crazy!"

"What? We're both dressed for it. Join me." He grinned at her mischievously.

"Okay," She took a tentative step into the water. "Oh, it's so warm. It's delicious."

Once she was fully immersed, Casey came up to her with the tray of strawberries.

"Want one?"

She nodded as Casey picked one up and fed it to her. Her lips grazed his fingertips, and his eyes closed, relishing the sensation.

"Here. Let me return the favor." She picked a strawberry and placed it in his mouth. His tongue darted forth and licked her fingers before biting the strawberry. The juice of the fruit ran down her fingers. He captured her hand, preventing retreat, and sucked every drop of juice away. Chaundra's breathing became heavy as her breasts heaved up and down.

"You know what's more breathtaking? You." Casey whispered, pushing the fruit onto the side of the pool and pulling Chaundra into a kiss. This kiss was different from the last time. There was an instant intensity, tingling from head to toe, from every bit of skin. Without thinking, Chaundra's legs found themselves wrapped around his waist, aligned with his firm manhood. Her arms wrapped around his neck, fingers running through his hair. He walked them to a built-in bench and sat down as he deepened the kiss. Chaundra's hips rocked against his, and he met her movements, rolling with her body. The sound of the water lapping against their skin intensified the experience. When they needed to breathe, finally, they pulled away from each other.

"Well, maybe Mr. Pfeiffer was on to something." Chaundra giggled.

"Well, there is a reason he's in charge. I guess, as good employees, we should listen to him." Casey turned his head back toward the bungalow.

"Satin, huh?" Chaundra grinned.

"He did say we should enjoy ourselves."

Chapter Twenty-One

NIGHTS LIKE SATIN

Casey carried Chaundra inside and headed toward the bed.

"Maybe, maybe we should wash that chlorine off? Shower?"

"Great idea, Chaundie," Casey redirected them toward the spa shower. He turned the water on to let it warm up. "You are so beautiful."

He trailed kisses down her shoulder and pulled the main string on her bikini top. It fell to the ground. His lips found their way to those delicious Hershey kiss nipples that topped the peaks of her abundant breasts. His tongue licked and sucked at them tentatively until he heard her breath hitch. Then, he really began his masterful assault on her breasts. He held her breast reverently, realizing that he was suckling a goddess.

"Case!" she gasped.

He grasped her butt, pulling her closer to his body. He needed every inch of her to touch him. The steam of the shower heated the room. Reluctantly, he took a final pull on her breasts and carried her into the shower.

Chaundra wanted to give as good as she was getting and took charge for a moment. She guided him to the shower seat and ran her hands over his chest. Casey loved that she was a take-charge kind of woman. He sat back and let her take the reigns for a while, enjoying the sight of her enthusiasm. She kissed his neck and his chest and worked her way down, kissing his abs, licking and biting each ridge. Her kisses led her down to his pubic mound and the large throbbing appendage that was aimed right at her. She grinned, knowing that it was all for her. She kissed down the length of his rod. Casey couldn't look away. Would she, could she let her lips wrap around him just the way that he wanted her to? He knew he couldn't let that happen. Not yet. His excitement was so great that it would end everything too soon, and there was so much more that he wanted to give to her before the night ended.

"Come here," Casey's ragged voice reached Chaundra's ears before she dove all the way in. He stood and brought her up along with him. He wrapped his arms around her, kissing her long and hard. Letting his tongue tell the story of what he planned to do to her entire body for the rest of the evening. Hot water ran over their flush bodies.

"Think we washed away enough chlorine?"

They dried each other off, lingering on the titillating body parts for longer than they needed. After, they ran giggling to the bed.

Their bodies slide against the coolness of the satin. Casey slid down her body until he got to her feet.

"You've been on these all day. Let me give them some attention." He began massaging her feet, watching for when her body became pliant. He kissed his way up her inner leg, nibbling as he bent her knee and spread her legs wide. He continued to kiss her leg and massage her foot until he reached her delicious center. He let his mouth cherish her folds intimately, savoring the taste of her excitement. He guided her other leg up until that knee was bent, too. He rubbed both of her feet simultaneously as he continued to provide oral pleasure. Chaundra could barely handle all of the sensations, and her lower half bucked against his face. He placed her legs over both shoulders and clutched her hips in his hands as his tongue pummeled her clitoris, and he became drunk off of her essence.

"Now, Casey. I need you."

That was all he needed to hear. He lined himself up at her entrance and thrust himself halfway, waiting for her body to relax. Even at that depth, her walls clenched him, pulling him further in.

"Yes, Casey!"

He thrust all the way in, driving himself in and out of Chaundra, rotating his hips until he knew she could feel just how much he wanted her, how grateful he was to be with her. He wanted her to know and feel everything he felt.

"You're everything I never knew I could have." He thrust into her again. Her body bowed off of the bed. "You're better than anyone I could have dreamed of."

Tears of pleasure and joy slipped from Chaundra's eyes. She rocked her hips up to meet his.

"I'm sorry I resisted. I want you." Casey shuddered at her words. "I want to be with you. I think I love you."

"I already love you."

His words pushed her over into a shuddering climax. It drove him to the point of ecstasy, shouting out her name over and over.

Epilogue

Two days, delivered meals, and many orgasms later, Casey and Chaundra were awakened by a knocking at the bungalow door.

"Chaundra! Are you still sick?" Rachael's voice called.

"Quick, get dressed," Chaundra said as she roused Casey.

"I'll be right there. Give me a second." Chaundra scrambled to pick their undergarments off the floor and tidy up. She started to head to the door when she heard Casey hiss at her.

"Chaundie! Robe!"

"Oh, goodness!" She had almost opened the door naked. Clothing had become so tertiary after that first session, and it was so comfortable and natural being naked around each other that she had forgotten that she needed to dress. After grabbing her robe and making sure Casey made it to the bathroom, she opened the door a crack.

"Damn, are you feeling that sick? It took you forever." Rachael asked.

"What? Um, yeah, sure. I mean, we're fine now."

"Wait a minute. Wait one hot minute. Let me look at you. You're glowing. You are absolutely radiant!"

Chaundra blushed. "I have no idea what you're talking about."

"Oh, don't play that with me again. I know what I see. Were you even sick?"

Chaundra just smirked. "Anyway, what can I do for you this morning?"

"Can I come in? I don't want all of my business out in the street."

Chaundra glanced behind her, making sure Casey was out of sight.

"Come on in."

Rachael stepped inside, took in the rumpled bed sheets, and started laughing.

"Oh, it's like that? Well, I won't keep you too long. I'm glad you two finally got there."

"Yeah," Chaundra blushed. "Me too. So, what's going on?"

"It's Peter. Ever since the fight, he's changed. He's less brazen. Quiet even."

"Well, that should be refreshing."

"It is, but..." Rachael trailed off.

"But?"

"He's also started following me around like a lost puppy. It's intense. He's actually a lot nicer than I thought."

"That sounds like a good thing, for the most part. So, what's the problem?"

Rachael chewed her bottom lip. Clearly, she was torn with what she was about to say.

"Well?"

"I think I like him!" Rachael blurted out and quickly covered her mouth in embarrassment.

At that moment, Casey stepped out of the restroom, fully clothed.

"Like who?" Casey asked.

There was another knock at the bungalow door.

"Rachael! Are you okay, sweet cheeks? Don't hide from me!" Peter's pleading voice could be heard through the door.

"What's he doing here?" Casey asked.

"Sorry, I'll go," Rachael said and headed to the door.

"You'll be alright. We'll talk later today," Chaundra said as she walked Rachael out. "Kisses."

She shut the door behind her and turned back to Casey's questioning face.

"Don't even ask. Let's just say I think Mr. Hendrick Pfeiffer isn't done matchmaking."

"The only match I care about right now is here in this room." He reached out, pulling her close and undoing the belt of her robe. "I think we need to see if that match still works. What do you think?"

Chaundra answered by kissing him until they fell back in bed. Nobody, least of all Mr. Pfeiffer, would mind if they didn't make it to the next team-building activity.

* * *

When Casey and Chaundra missed the next activity, Hendrick stood like a proud papa. "Success #1, Kathy. Who's next?" he asked. He threw back his head and bubbled over with laughter. Yes, Mr. Hendrick Pfeiffer, CEO, was very satisfied indeed.

Stay tuned for Peter and Rachael's story.

Acknowledgments

Thank you to the following AMAZING authors and industry professionals who contributed their knowledge and time, providing me with education and inspiration:
Eva O'Hare, Pepper Pace, Posey Parks, AR Williams, Jailaa West, Carla Truss, Joseph Federico, Reana Malori, Harper Black, Octavia Price, Lynette Angelica Sivad, Eliza Lovejay, Philly Loves Romance, and The Sunday Romance Writers.
Special thanks to Editor and Cheerleader Extraordinaire, Tori Moore. You have gone above and beyond to make my debut and final manuscript an amazing experience. Your expertise and guidance have been invaluable. You are so very much appreciated. Thank you.
Finally, much love and thanks to my family and friends, especially my wonderfully supportive husband, T.

About the Author

Ruby D. Flowers has been writing and creating movies in her mind since she was a small child entertaining herself while doing chores. She has written several children's plays, performed, directed, acted, sang and even danced (questionably, if not adequately) on stage and film. Her love of comedy, the absurd, and a happy ending has drawn her to romantic comedy. After all, what is living but a series of absurd and unexpected situations that lead us through life and love? We might as well have a laugh at the whole experience.